Random
Conversations

Random
Conversations

HERBERT

PARTRIDGE
A Penguin Company

Partridge books may be ordered through booksellers or by contacting:

Partridge India
Penguin Books India Pvt.Ltd
11, Community Centre, Panchsheel Park, New Delhi 110017
India
www.partridgepublishing.com
Phone: 000.800.10062.62

Contents

Dedicated to college students across the globe

Introduction

'What is this waste stack of paper lying here? Shall I give it off to the paper wala?' my mother yelled.

'What is this? Everything you just want to give off to the paper wala? My record books, project books, everything. Any paper in the house, you want to sell it off!'

'What are you going to do with all this? When you had to study from those books itself you won't open and see.As if now after joining work you will open and study? You want to show your grandchildren or what? Simply accumulating rubbish in the house. At least this paper wala will give me money for this waste.'

'OK, OK. Give it off. Don't simply shout.One day sell me also to the paper wala.'

'He won't buy.'

She smiled mouth wide open. My mother thinks by giving away books and paper, half her burden of cleaning the house is done.

'WAIT. Wait. Show me that.' I pulled the stack of paper off her hands.

She huffed in frustration and left the room. Mumbling to herself, she went away to clean the kitchen.

I recognized the writing on those sheets of paper. On top of the sheet, my sister had scribbled in large bold font

"If you publish this, everybody will forget their English. DO NOT PUBLISH. Do not destroy this world. YOU WILL REGRET IT."

*　　*　　*

I had made a compilation of all the conversations I had with my friends in school and college and as if I had written the greatest of novels ever in the history of mankind, I showed it to my sister for proofreading.

'Read this. This is my first novel. It is really great!' I beamed with joy.

She read the first chapter.

'Yuck' she spat at me. 'You call this a novel?'

'Hey! Why? Is it not good?'

'GOOD? Are you out of your mind? This is the worst piece of rubbish I have ever read in my life.'

'Shall we publish it?'

'Can't you understand me you fool?'

She angrily scribbled on a piece of paper and threw the papers at me.

*　　*　　*

In time I got busy with work and forgot about my novel. Now I was holding the first draft in my hand. I looked at that note and laughed.

I dialed my sister's number.

'Ya, tell me. What's up?' She asked unassumingly.

'I'm going to publish it.' I proclaimed.

'Publish what?' At first she was confused. 'OH MY GOD. Have you lost your mind? Mental. Crack pot. That stupid book is still in the house? I'll ask mummy to throw it . . . idiot . . . that good for nothing . . .'

And she continued yelling.

I was smiling at the other end. No matter what she told me, I had made up my mind.

Prologue

'Oh! Look who's up so early!' My mother exclaimed as she served *masala dosa* to my father. 'Where are you going?'

'To the church, mom'

'I heard from someone that these days children go to temples and churches only during results time,' she stopped for a minute. "who was it . . . ?" she thought.

'Chutney?' My dad asked. She served chutney quickly to my father, who looked least interested in anything but his plate. 'So the results are expected today, is it?'

'Why do you say that? You think I am not holy?' I defended myself. 'I also heard from someone that old people are always saying dumb and imaginary things . . .' I put on my shoes quickly 'who told me that . . . I wonder . . . hmmm'

'Make fun. Make fun of your own mother.' She looked at me.

I looked away.

I, Justin Zachariah, had written my state board examinations two months ago and got unconfirmed reports that the result would be out anytime today. I was the only child in my family and had no siblings.

'If you go correctly during results time God will not give you state first.' My mom, Sara Zachariah proclaimed. 'You should have gone regularly during exam time.' She was the head of the bible group in St. Luke's Church, my parish. 'When will you ever listen to me? If I had another child, may be that would have.' She went into mummy senti mode.

'Chutney?' My dad asked again.

I took my bicycle and rode quickly out of my house. The road was empty and the air was clean. It was 7 in the morning and the world was into the third week of May in 2005. I was born and brought up in the city of Chennai. My parents migrated from Kerala when I was hardly 3 months old. I did not know Malayalam. The only occasion when I use the term *Mallu* (Malayalis are fondly referred to as *Mallus*) is when I am among a few good looking girls from Kerala. And Chennai had lots of them.

I peddled for a few minutes across the empty streets to reach the church in my neighborhood. My longtime foe, Jeffrey, stood inside the church campus, smiling as I entered.

'Is the information true?' I asked.

'You have come to church. Then it must be true.' Jose and Matthew stood close to Jeffrey. 'How happy am I to see you here!'

'So what time is it expected?'

'Why are you bothered? I heard that you have already blocked your seat in St. Patrick College of Engineering.' He scorned. 'So these results matter little to you.'

'Hey you know dude. Sometimes I wonder why people call me a dumbass.' I said with disgust. 'I am standing here and asking a kid, who pees in bed, questions.' I replied.

'Did it take so many wasted years for you to understand that you are a dumbass?' He said angrily.

'And I do not pee in bed, you ignorant fool!' Jeffrey came closer, almost about to hit me. But one advantage of being in India is that most fights do not usually kick off into a physical fight. We try and act all tough and usually resort to verbal abuses.

'Dude the information is true.' Jose interrupted, knowing that the conversation was going nowhere.

I hated Jeffrey. He hated me more.

Standing tall at 173cms, Jeffrey was over 72 kgs in weight and was proud of his long moustache and unshaved beard. He was holy in public and spread the good news of God whenever possible. He was also an integral part of the bible group at St. Luke's Church.

'Shouldn't you be conducting the mass now, FATHER?' I teased Jeffrey.

'Not funny.' Jose replied as Jeffrey stared at me with anger. 'This is a church. Control your tongue.'

'I understand.' I said as Jeffrey kept staring at me.

I went inside the church, closed my eyes, prayed for a few seconds, got up silently and sat on one of the pews.

I was not a smart student who could score the 95s or 100s required to clear an IIT or a state level university.

Citing my limitations as a student, my father, Andrew Zachariah, paid few lakhs in St. Patrick College of Engineering, for a seat in computer science engineering (every private college in Chennai had 50% seats reserved for the management who sold it to students like me who could afford to get into a college ONLY with the help of money).

I sat there silently thinking about money and its power. Not that I was bothered about the world and the people suffering here, but I was concerned about what this money could do.

I sat thinking about what was in store for me if I actually screwed up in my paper. I knew a lot of people were waiting for my failure in this exam.

Chapter 1

My First Foe

Jeffrey was my class mate from 4th grade and my best buddy till the 11th grade, until one day he became my dreaded foe. Dreaded, in my term, did not mean he wanted to kill me, but simply meant that he kept disturbing me in social websites, class rooms and in private birthday parties, which is dreaded for kids like me who are active online and offline.

*   *   *

January 2004:

"'You know what.'

'What?'

'Do you know the best thing to happen in my life?' Jeffrey asked me.

'Is it your ability to masturbate?'

'That can't be the best thing to happen in anyone's life!' Jeffrey explained. 'Every kid loves till it spills out in his pants!' The hard truth, I thought. 'The best thing to happen in my life is today.' He whispered in my ears. 'I am alive to see this day.' He smiled happily.

'What's so special about today?' I asked.

'Dude! We are standing outside this school.' Jeffrey replied.

We were standing outside Krishna H.S.S waiting for the watchman to permit us inside so that we could go and attend the cultural competitions inside.

I turned and stared hard into the eyes of the aging fat watchman.

'Yes, and we will keep standing outside until this crack pot does not let us in. WE ARE FROM DB SCHOOL' I yelled.

'I need your ID card.' The watchman replied coolly

'ID Card vanthu odane onuku appu da.' *(I will screw you as soon as I get my ID card)*

The watchman did not give a damn of what I said.

'Dude, look at the positive side.'

'Please enlighten me, O great one!'

'We are not alone.'

If Jeffrey meant not alone, he meant girls.

I turned around and saw a girl, possibly of the same age as Jeffrey and me, standing at the extreme end of the gate, with her two other girls of the same age. She was short in height and had a tanned look. She was thin and had long curly hair. 'She looks good.'

'Now you are talking.' Jeffrey smiled. 'Let's look at things that might happen in the next few immediate minutes.'

'Go on, I am listening.'

'Situation 1: She will be bored standing at the gate in a few minutes and so will come to us, will chat for a few minutes and eventually we will become good friends.'

'I don't think that will happen.'

'Situation 2: She will feel hungry and would like to have something but she forgot to bring her purse.'

'So?'

'So I will buy her something and we will become friends.'

'Possible, but you will face stiff competition. Do not forget that there are other guys next to us who are probably planning to do the same thing.' I informed. 'Rule me out of the race. I have only 20 bucks in my pocket and would like to strictly use it for food only.'

'Situation 3: She will faint because of sun stroke and we will go and help her.'

'I don't think any of this will happen.'

'Why do you say that?'

'The Watchman already sent her in along with her friends.' The watchman opened the gate and let the girls in.

'Oh' Jeffrey was disappointed.

I laughed at him.

'Sir' Jeffrey asked the watchman. 'You got the confirmation from our school that we are students there?'

'No. The school chief informed us that he has never heard about you guys before.'

'But we are from DB school. Why would the chief say that?'

'I did call DB school. Ask your chief, Mr. Ram, why he said that. You guys can now leave.'

'Mr. Ram? Sir but our chief's name is Stephen.'

'You guys don't even know your chief's name?'

'Sir we know for sure our chief is Stephen. He has been the chief for over 15 years in DB School.'

'That's a surprise.' The watchman thought. 'The attendant of the call stated that Mr. Ram has also been in DB for 15 years.'

'Which DB school are you talking about?'

'David Boy's School!'

*   *   *

'I promise you all a glass of mango juice if I score above 90' boasted Jeffrey, as we stepped out of the church. 'Which I think I will'

'I will be happy if I touch 75.' Jose stated.

'Me too' I replied and quickly turned to Jeffrey. 'But I will be much happier if I score more than you.'

'That you won't' He replied stiffly.

'That I might'

'How so?'

'Don't forget your second language is German and you will easily go down with it.'

'Ah . . . in your dreams! I have mastered that language.'

'Mastered it by mixing it with French! If the staff knows both German and French, you will score high.' I laughed out loud.

'You know that is not funny.' Jeffrey roared.

'If you feel bad when someone teases you, then why do you tease others?' I shouted back.

'Fuck you. I just don't want to be teased by an idiot like you.'

*　　*　　*

January 2004:

"You know, for winning in this competition we will have to act out dumb and should also be funny.'

'Now that's funny.' Jeffrey chuckled. 'So that is what people call as role playing eh?'

'Exactly'

'I am ok with acting funny but not dumb. I don't think I have to win here by losing my prestige.'

'Ok.' I informed Jeffrey. We finally got into Krishna H.S.S after the watchman confirmed with Stephen about us. We were sent by our school cultural department to participate in the "role playing" competition in this school, simply because the rest of the DB school representatives were busy attending the cultural competition in Lady Andal School, which was supposedly the best cultural festival conducted in Chennai.

Cultural competitions were organized round the year in various schools, in and around India. Usually conducted in a span of two to three days, it was a good reason to miss school classroom life.

Jeffrey and I knocked at the doors of the cultural organizers for over 3 years to get an opportunity to get a feel of what participating in cultural competitions actually felt and were finally given the opportunity to participate in this school, beating off stiff competition from no one!

'We were given the opportunity to participate in this school simply because no one else wanted to participate here.' I informed Jeffrey. 'But something is better than nothing.'

'Very true and this opportunity is better than anything!'

Role playing was a competition which made to the list of any cultural competition simply because the event was funny and creative. Every participant had to act out like a famous celebrity (ex. Gandhiji or Sachin Tendulkar), giving reasons why he is the most important person in the list of celebrities. Every school varied their rules and style of organizing this event, but ultimately what mattered to the participants was winning.

It differed from Ship Wreck (another famous event conducted as part of cultural competitions), as it dealt with reasons as to why the celebrity and not others, should be saved from the sinking ship. Role playing on the other hand, dealt more with stating reasons as to why that particular celebrity is better than the rest and should be considered as the best person to have ever lived (or living) in this world.

Here, in Krishna H.S.S, the participants were given 2 minutes to enact the given character, and each team comprised of two participants from the same school. They had to fight it out among each other to prove to the audience that one is better than the other. Like "Osama Bin Laden" tipped against "George Bush".

'I will be happy to get David Beckham. Always wanted to step into his shoes and feel what it felt like to him. Who do you want to be?' Jeffrey asked me eagerly.

'Steve Jobs.'

'Who is he?'

'He is the owner of Apple.'

'You want to be an apple vendor? That's funny.'

I stared at Jeffrey for a moment and replied 'No wonder people say Microsoft has spoilt our nation.'

'The participants from Don Bosco School are requested to come on stage.' The emcee announced.

'We must have brought a camera man to shoot what we are going to do on stage.' Jeffrey said as we got up from our place and started walking towards the stage. 'At least a few friends would have spoken about us in school.'

'Spoken about what?'

'About us running away with the winner's trophy in Role playing'

'I will say we are lucky we have made it so far' I informed Jeffrey. 'Practically speaking we are very lucky!'

'Why do you say that? You think we will lose?'

'You don't know what it is to be on stage, do you?'

'All the world's a stage, my friend.' Jeffrey spoke out loud.

'Let me see you tell that after a few minutes.'

We took center stage and I smiled at the audience. Jeffrey had never participated in any cultural competition (I participated in the fancy dress competition for 5 consecutive years, dressed as a police officer) prior to this day and he did not know what it took to be there. He slowly started showing signs of uneasiness as fear crept into his nerves.

'I feel odd and awkward.' He whispered. 'What is happening to me?'

'It's called stage fear.' I replied swiftly. 'It happens to most of us.'

'Why is it not happening to you?'

'Cause I have already experienced it few weeks ago in school when they told me to hold the prop on stage for the annual day play.'

'Ah! I remember one of the trees collapsed.'

'That was me.'

'The characters given to you two are' The judge informed '"Elton John" and "The lion King". You will be given 30 seconds to decide on what you want to talk and then both of you will go live. Your time starts now.'

'Now she has got to my nerves. Who is Elton John?' Jeffrey trembled in fear.

'He is a singer who sang for the movie "The lion king".'

'Then I must reprise that role. You be the lion king.'

'Ok.'

'Time's up. You can start acting.'

'I . . . I am a great singer and I am . . . eh . . . . am the one man in this world that everyone wants to beee . . . be like' Jeffrey did not start out brightly.

'That is the dumbest thing I have heard as the whole world believes that you are gay. I don't think all men want to be gay.' The crowd clapped and Jeffrey was stunned.

'I . . . I am noo . . . ot gay.'

'Ah! I must be a dumb ass to believe that. I am the king of the jungle and the savior of all animals. The world needs me and my power and not gays like you.'

Jeffrey was shocked and stared around the hall. Everyone backed me by chanting my name, making Jeffrey feel out of place. It was a known fact among all who knew Jeffrey that he was one man who did not like to be insulted in public. He had plenty of pride for a guy aging 16. He did not talk further and walked off from the stage, 60 seconds prior to the completion of the event.

'As your team mate has left the stage, you will not be allowed to complete the event. Thank you!' the judge informed, as I followed Jeffrey down the stage.

'Dude, why the hell did you walk off?' I asked Jeffrey quickly.

'Why the hell did you call me a gay?' Jeffrey roared back.

'I called Elton John a gay, not you. You must not take what happens there on stage seriously.'

'You insulted me in front of 1000 people? How could you?'

'Don't think there were 1000. Must be 875 to 900'

'And then you tell me not to take it seriously? Do you think I am out of my mind to take this as a joke?' Jeffrey roared back. 'You think I am a fool?'

'Dude . . .'

'Fuck you.'

*　　*　　*

'That guy is an emotional fucker.' Jose told me. Jose and I took our respective bicycles and left the church while Matthew left with Jeffrey. We drove to a nearby tea stall for a cup of tea and a plate of samosa. 'He always reacts to any stupid joke you tell.'

'That was the main reason why he became my enemy.' I said sadly. 'You know I thought time will resolve the problem, but it has been over a year since that issue took place and surprisingly Jeffrey still hates me.'

*　　*　　*

March 2004 :

'Dude why are you avoiding me? You know I did not do it intentionally. Can't you take it as a joke and forget it.' I was finally able to get Jeffrey on the phone, after his mother forced him to talk with me.

'I will forgive an enemy, but not a friend who stabs me from the back.'

'That's so dumb.'

'Dumb people do not understand feelings.' Jeffrey roared. 'I only wanted to avoid you, but now I hate you. Just you see; I will ensure that you don't sleep anymore in the coming days.'

'Don't be stupid dude. It's more like waging a war over a nation for the death of the queen who had an affair with someone else.'

'Majority of the wars in the past were fought for girls.'

'Hmmm . . . And for someone who was not even a virgin. Surprising they went to the extent of building a massive horse to destroy a nation, all for a runaway wife!'

'Fuck you.'

*   *   *

'I have not seen a lot of people who hate their friends for stupid reasons like the one you mentioned.' Jose replied.

'I asked for forgiveness whenever I met him in 11th and 12th grade, but he never forgave me. Now I am least bothered about him.'

'You told me that. Now if he seriously scores less than you in the board exams, he is going to curse you big time and blame you for his underperformance.'

'Don't you think his father would have surely bought him a seat in some college?'

'I am sure he already would have. And I am also sure that his performance in the board exams will be pathetic.'

'I surely hope he does not end up with me in St. Patrick College of Engineering.'

'You never know, he actually might.' Jose smiled. 'But tell me one thing; do you know anyone else who has blocked a seat in that college, other than you, from our school?'

'I was informed by Jones' father that he got a seat for him in the same department.' Jones was my school mate, and a very annoying school mate I should say. His only objective in school was to observe me and my activities, day in and out, and inform his dad about everything that turned dirty on my side. His dad, in turn, informed my dad about it, hoping I'd get some bashing. It's a vicious cycle.

'hmm, anybody else?'

'People don't like to talk about the fact that they had to pay for their seats, right?'

'Right'

*   *   *

'Hi'

I finally reached my house by 9'o clock in the morning and found a young guy seated there, someone (I assume) of the same age as mine. He was dark, had no moustache, sported spiked hair and stood almost 182 cms tall. He was close to 90 kgs in weight and looked more like a bouncer. I did not know what to talk to him or even his intentions of visiting my place. *Was he a hit man sent by Jeffrey to kill me? Naaa . . . Jeffrey won't waste money for that!*

'Hi.' I said and he quickly smiled. I was really happy to see him smiling. *He was not there to kick my ass!*

'This is Chris.' My mother said, as she served him a cup of coffee. 'Coffee for you, Justin?'

'Nah . . . I had tea from Mahesh's tea stall.'

'I heard that they make the tea with dirty water.' My mother looked concerned.

'According to you, everything I eat from outside is made with dirty water and in dirty dishes.'

My mother just looked blankly at me and said 'Chris is joining you in your college.'

'Oh! Great' I said

'Yes' Chris smiled 'I finished my schooling in Bangalore and so am not eligible for applying via scholarship for any college in Tamil Nadu. I had to buy a seat in St. Patrick College' He smiled.

'My son did not have to worry about.' My mother interrupted. 'He was not eligible for scholarship before he even took up his exams.' I did not reply as my mother continued. 'By the way, your grandparents were saying that you are going to stay here till you finish college?'

'Yes aunty.' He replied 'Excuse me for a minute' Chris answered his mobile as he walked out.

'Why do you always have to say insignificant things to people?' I yelled at my mother

'He will anyway find out.' She replied. 'You will be happy to know that he marginally cleared his papers in his board exams in Bangalore. His results were announced last week and he scored only 60%. His parents have come down to Chennai to pay extra for the seat that they blocked, cause he did not get 75%.'

People scoring 75% were termed eligible to be an engineer.

'So that means even if I don't get the required 75%, I can save the seat by paying extra bucks.' I was relieved to get that information. Now I knew why the prospectus read "conditions apply".

'No if you don't get the 75%, we will ask for a refund and push you to some random arts college in our native place.' My mother informed me. 'You know what it is to study in our native right? You have to speak in Malayalam!'

'No. Thanks.'

'Sorry aunty, I had to attend an important call.' Chris walked back in.

'No issues son.' My mother replied as she saw the clock quickly. 'It is 10'o clock now. Check the net if the results are out.'

'Let's wait for a few minutes.' I said. 'I don't think we will be able to connect because everybody will be on the net now.'

'I am already online son.' My father, a chartered accountant in a leading private firm in Chennai, shouted out. 'Give me your number.'

'Hmmm . . .' I started shivering. 'It is 587645'

'Ok.'

He typed the number and the results popped up **1134/1200**.

'Awesome you rocked.' Chris congratulated me.

'Thanks' I roared in joy '94.5% overall! I am on top of the world.'

'Good for Harish Charan.' My father said.

'Harish Charan?'

'Yes. Harish Charan. Because this is his marks. Give me your number, Mr. Justin Zachariah.'

'587644'

'Ok.' I prayed to God silently as Chris slowly got up from his place and signaled a thumbs up at me.

'Hmmm . . . I am surprised.' My father said slowly

'He passed?' My mother asked nervously

'Better.' My father looked very happy. 'Though unbelievable, these are certainly your marks.'

'He crossed 75%?' My mother squealed.

'No. He scored 1041/1200. That's 86.75%.'

'Wow!' I roared in joy as Chris patted my back.

'Congratulations, dude!'

'Thanks man. Finally my hard work pays off!'

'Ah! My son talking about hard work disturbs me.' My father said.

I went towards the PC, closely followed by Chris, to check my subject wise performance.

'It is official dude. You are going to spend your 4 years of engineering life in St. Patrick College of Engineering.'

Chapter 2

A new friend

Present-June 2005:

'So you are taking me to college, aren't you?' I asked my parents quickly. It was the 1st week of June, that time of the year when colleges were flooded by confirmation letters from students who had blocked their seats.

I was getting dressed up to go to St. Patrick College of Engineering, to submit my documents and mark sheets and may be signing a few agreements to commit myself to joining there.

'No.' My father replied

'So how do you expect me to go?'

'Here.' My father handed over a new wallet to me.

'A new wallet!'

'Yes. Check inside'

'10 Rupees!' I was disappointed.

'Yes. That should be enough for you to go and come back from college.'

'I don't even know where my college is. How do you expect me to go and come back safely?'

'You need not worry about that.' My father informed. 'Chris will be accompanying you. In fact, he was the one who recommended us not to accompany you guys. He wants to travel in a bus to get the feel of going to college on a daily basis via bus.'

'Why do we have to get used to that? I thought you guys were planning to drop and pick me from college on a daily basis.'

'Your college rule says "bus mandatory".'

'Great.' I sighed as Chris came in. 'How about adding a few extra bucks for lunch and snacks there?'

'We should be back for lunch.' Chris replied.

For over two weeks, I got to know a lot about Chris, simply because he was the only person available to accompany me to the movies.

I got to know one thing about him: he was clearly not the type of person I expected him to be. He was innocent and soft spoken. He was not a person who got himself into trouble but a person who kept a good distance away from trouble.

'You ready, Justin?' He was neatly dressed for the long travel in bus.

'Yes!' I said in an angry tone.

'Great. Hurry up or else we will miss the 10:00 am bus to college.' He checked his watch quickly. 'We should be there by 11:00am, complete the formalities by 12:00pm and be back by 1:00pm.'

*   *   *

'You know what' Chris started as we boarded the 21H bus that headed straight to our college campus. 'I was forced to pay extra 2 lakhs for the seat in our college, only because I scored 60%.'

'Sad' I replied.

'I am not coming to that.' Chris said. 'I saw Babuji there with his son.'

'The famous social activist?' I was curious to know more. 'He came to my school and spoke on the topic *The need to eradicate corruption.*'

'His son had got just 55% and Babuji was present there to pay 5 lakhs extra so that his son would not lose the seat! Crazy right?'

'Yes. And Babuji talks in public against corruption!' Expected from people who talk against corruption 'I even believed him to be an angel from heaven!' I smiled. 'At least the women who accompanied him looked like angels from heaven!'

'They must be his "followers". And he drives around the city in a Rolls Royce Ghost.'

'What a man!'

'But tell me one thing, Justin. On a serious note, I have been here in Chennai for over two weeks now and the only access to information about Chennai for me is you and my grandparents.'

'Yes.'

'My grandparents took me to places as boring and old as them. But you have not yet shown me places where I would love to be.'

'I did take you to beaches and a few malls.'

'That's crap. I mean business.'

'You mean IT company?'

'No. I mean places where chicks come.'

'Hmmm! I thought you were a good kid.'

'We are men and we must follow chicks. Following them does not make us bad.'

'Wow!'

'I needed time to reveal myself.' Chris smiled out. 'And I don't talk a lot too. I prefer being myself only to people whom I can trust.'

'Oh! So you trust me?'

'I don't have a choice'

'Now that you are talking in my language, I am going to help you in the best way possible.' I smiled out.

'Great!' Chris' eyes glittered.

'But what would you do when we actually go to places where chicks flood?'

Chris came closer. 'What else? Like 9 out of 10 guys in India do, sit and watch them have fun, take a picture with them in the background, and irritate all our friends in Hi5 by uploading the picture with a tag "I was there"'

'Dude!'

*   *   *

'This is what I am talking about.' I said with my mouth wide open. We reached the college campus in an hour and got down in front of a massive building, constructed with at least 15 floors. 'And they call it a "college office"! Bloody this is better than the IT companies flooding the city.'

There were 12 buildings constructed around the massive administrative building: 9 engineering departments occupying 1 building each and 3 buildings allotted for labs and workshop. There was a huge canteen constructed and the college canteen had the capacity to serve for 2000 students at the same time. Standing tall, a few metres away, was a huge auditorium, with a capacity to seat the entire college.

'Dude' Chris started 'The whole area is networked together.'

'No wonder they charge so much for each and every seat they sell.' I said 'They probably built these buildings with the money they collected from our seniors.'

We walked into the administrator's office quickly. There were over 25 students present there, some alone and most girls accompanied by their parents.

'You know the reason why parents pay in lakhs to send their daughters to this college.' Chris said. 'Because they know that the probability of their daughter falling in love with a boy here is apparently lesser than in any other college.'

'Why do you say that?' I asked quickly.

'What do you think college life is for? Studies, grades and eventually placements? My friend, college is one open matrimonial site where guys and girls can choose their life partner from! These St. Patrick's guys are totally against this.'

'Sounds interesting'

'Have you not heard about "deathrimony" in this college?' He asked.

'What is that?'

'If you want to get friendly with a girl in our college, the college officials will kill you. Meaning, you will eventually get married to death!'

'Wow.'

'Let me explain it to you. There is this portal in St. Patrick called SMS.'

'SMS?'

'Speak Management System. You will have to raise a request in that portal by filling details like:

1. Who you want to speak to?
2. The reason for the request.
3. Your ID, name and other details.
4. Expected time of discussion

Once it gets approved, which in most cases doesn't, you will be allotted a place in the administrative office where you will have to come at the specified time and discuss all that you want.'

'That's dumb'

'Yes. And if you try breaking the rules, they will relocate your balls.' Chris warned.

'But there is still a probability of guys getting the girls into their love net.' I smiled. 'For every problem, there is a solution.'

'It's up to the guys.'

'You know what. Colleges are known for cultural competitions also.'

'Culturals? What is that?'

'You seriously don't know what cultural competitions are? It is "the thing" in college life.'

'Tell me more.'

'Schools conducted cultural competitions so that people bring out their hidden talent. In College, winners of cultural competitions are respected like Gods. As in, you will feel like a member of the Arsenal Invincible team.'

'Oh. And what are the events that are conducted as part of cultural competitions in college?'

'Starting from dancing, singing to events like debate, dramatics, face painting, gaming, coding, paper presentation, and so. You name it, and cultural competitions have it.'

'Oh!'

'And what's more, it is the hunting ground for good looking girls too.'

'Wow! Now college life is getting interesting.'

'I know. If we miss out on any girl here in our college, we can compensate by finding a better girl there.'

'It sounds exciting. And with deathrimony active here, we will mostly have to look out for girls outside our campus' Chris smiled.

'So you have already accepted defeat?'

'I have decided not to play the game in the first place.' He informed swiftly.

We were directed into a room, where we sat in the second row with our documents in our hand. Suddenly, as if my worst dream had come true, my foe walked in.

'Jeffrey?' I said to myself as I saw Jeffrey grinning at me. He was accompanied by his father, and so kept a fair amount of distance from me.

'You know him?'

'He is my enemy.'

'Enemy? What did he do against you?'

*   *   *

August 2004:

'"Justin, come here.' My chemistry ma'am, Mrs. Sandra called out to me. 'What the hell is this?'

'What did I do ma'am?' I was shocked as she looked angry at me. I had never been caught in class for any mischievous activity and this was the first time that Sandra ma'am, who liked me and claimed that I was one of the best students in her class, caught me for some activity I was totally not aware of.

'Writing a letter like this to me?' She shouted out loud. 'You are so very dead.'

'Letter?' She showed a letter to me which read like this

Very soon women will pay men to suck their breasts! Doctors recommend that women reduce the risk of breast cancer by having their breast sucked. So ma'am to avoid getting cancer in the near future please let me suck your breast.

'Ma'am, seriously I did not write this.' I cried out loud.

'I never expected you to do this Justin. I thought you were a good kid.'

'Ma'am I am serious.'

'Give your reasons to the principal.'

She did not lend her ears to anything I said and took me straight to the principal. I was suspended for a month from school."

* * *

'Jeffrey seriously did that?' Chris asked me.

'He wanted to screw up my life and kept working against me.'

'But usually if someone writes a letter like that, they are usually thrown out of school permanently. How did you escape with a month suspension?'

'Cause the letter was in printed form and when my parents were summoned they informed the principal that I was a crackpot who was misguided by some mischievous kids.' I informed Chris. 'And most importantly my father took care of the school accounts.'

'Oh'

'Even my parents did not believe me. Jeffrey is a mad guy, at least for me.'

'He sure sounds like a loser. But why does he hate you in the first place?'

'It's a long story.'

'Tell me later then.'

'Looks like you have already made friends here.' Jeffrey stated cunningly. 'God save him.'

'He is my neighbor and our future class mate.' I replied. 'Looks like the dog came wagging its tail to the college where I joined.'

'I got a free seat.' Jeffrey replied

'Good one! You got only 1020/1200, that 85% and just 120 out of 200 in German which is a known fact to all around you.'

'Don't be friends with him.' Jeffrey informed Chris, opting not to reply for my statement. 'He will work against his own friends.'

'It amuses me to meet a person like you who complains to a person who never existed in your world just a few minutes back.' Chris looked straight into Jeffrey's eyes. 'I think I can believe Justin but not you.' Chris replied, enraging Jeffrey.

'Jeffrey, come here.' His father called as Jeffrey walked away from our place.

'Thanks for that.' I thanked Chris.

'He is definitely a loser. It is written all over his face.' Chris replied.

'You will make a good judge.' I smiled.

'I just need to see a person once. I will get a complete idea about who he/she is and what his/her character is.' Chris said proudly.

'Ah! I am just surprised that Jeffrey did not inform anyone that he bought a seat here.'

'I am sure he would have bought a seat in this college before we did.'

'I think you are right.'

'Justin, please come and submit your mark sheets.' The staff seated in the front desk called out my name as I got up from my place and walked towards her.

Chapter 3

Patcult

'**Y**ou must buy a mobile with an inbuilt camera.' Chris informed me.

'I am sorry Chris, as my budget will not allow me to spend anything more than 5000 rupees for a mobile.' I replied. 'And for your kind information, I have a camera.'

'Then you will have to settle for a black and white mobile.'

'That is exactly what I came looking for.'

'The girls won't be impressed.'

'I know. If only mobiles with cameras were available for my budget.'

'You will have to wait for 3 more years for that.' Chris informed. 'Actually I would say that waiting is not a bad option.'

'I agree'

'Sir' the shop keeper interrupted 'Which mobile are you opting for?'

'We will come tomorrow. I have not yet decided what to go for.' I replied.

'How many days is tomorrow Sir?'

'Eh?'

'80 out of 100 who say tomorrow end up coming after a year. So see you next year.'

I grinned and walked out of the store with Chris. Over the past few months, Chris and I visited majority of the malls and multiplexes. And no one accompanied us along as both of us were single (as far as I knew at the moment).

My experience today was different from any experience that I had previously, simply because it was my first day in college. My experience in St. Patrick was way different than what I had experienced back in school. For starters, there were girls in my classroom!

From the age of 4 to 17, I studied in a boys school. Girls came to our school, accompanied by their parents to pick up their brothers. Or they

The 2005-2009 CSE-A batch in St. Patrick College of Engineering comprised of 61 students. People from various geographic locations, starting from various states in India like Kerala, Andhra Pradesh, Tamil Nadu, Maharashtra etc. to various countries like Oman, Saudi Arabia, Malaysia and Bahrain were seated in the same place.

The classes in St. Patrick College were scheduled from 8 in the morning to 3 in the evening. One surprising aspect of our college was that students were not permitted to carry their food along with them, as breakfast, lunch and tea was served to all in the campus. And the funny part was that anyone who carried food along, if caught, would be penalized!

The dress code followed here was formals (black formal shoes, shirt and formal pants with white/black tie) for boys and chudidhar (Indian traditional attire) for girls. Even staffs were forced to wear blazers or formal suits to class and any staff found violating that rule would be penalized 30% of their daily's pay.

All students were forced to avail the bus facility provided by the college. With over 80 buses functioning all around the city, students were allowed to enter the college campus only if they were found in a college bus.

On the first day in college we had to attend an induction program, which spanned for over 3 hours. It gave us an insight about what we could (and should) expect during the four years in this college. After that we were taken for a campus tour, where we were introduced to all the facilities available in the college like the mess, the various department buildings, labs, classrooms, libraries, and our massive auditorium.

One thing that impressed me and grabbed my attention was the *patcult* program in college, one of the few programs (at the end of the induction program) that I was eagerly looking forward to.

Patcult was an initiative taken up in my college, to encourage students to participate in various cultural competitions in India. Anyone who enrolled with *patcult* would be sent to various colleges to participate in various events, with an On-Duty certificate. But it was also brought to my notice the staffs and student representatives had a major role to play in selecting the final list of students in the *patcult* initiative. On a brighter side, those who could not make it to the *patcult* association could make it into it by simply taking a gamble of taking a day off from college and attending the cultural events, and if the individual won in an event, he would be immediately included in the group.

But to remain in the group he/she must not lose in 3 consecutive cultural competitions, which would lead to he/she bring eliminated from the group. And he/she would have to eventually follow the same process as an outsider should to get back into it. So it was a dynamic group.

'Whether I make it to the final list of *patcult* or not, I am now really excited about the cultural competitions you were talking about.' Chris started.

'Why is that?' I asked him, as he stated exactly what I wanted him to say at that moment.

'I was seriously impressed during the induction program when they mentioned about *patcult*. And I get a feeling that it is our best bet to prove to the world we are super cool'

'Which we are not'

'Which we can be, if we try'

'You know I thought only we were single in this whole world. But after joining college, I have realized that it was the hand which has been doing the talking for almost everyone around us.'

'And with the ratio of girls to boys being something close to 1:10, I am sure we will not be able to compete against them.'

'I agree. I just realized that when ten guys fell to the ground when the girl in the front row . . .' I paused for a moment 'what was her name?'

'Priya'

'Yes, Priya' I continued 'When Priya dropped her handkerchief to the ground. Man I did not expect that from our guys!'

'I too did not expect that. Two of our guys got injured in the process.' Chris informed. 'You know what: the handkerchief was dirty when Fahd picked it up.'

'She was using it from the morning to clean her nose. Yuck!'

'Guys won't give a damn about that until the girls smile back.'

'And I would not take the risk of getting caught for hitting on a girl, simply because our college mission statement says *4 years in our college you will have to be single. If you think otherwise, we will have to mingle in your life to make you single!*

'Scary mission statement' Chris said

'I have some information for you which might interest you.'

'Tell me and let me decide whether it is interesting or not.'

'We can check girl's pictures in Orkut.'

'What is Orkut?'

'It is a social website where you can check out various girls' uploaded pictures and comments on it online, for the world to see.'

'Wow! But that is what we do in Hi5 also right?'

'How many times have you seen a girl fall in love with a boy and living happily ever after in bollywood?'

'Infinite.'

'I rest my case.' I smiled. 'Let's not compare two similar websites. But here are some features I would like to list down which might interest you.'

'Go on.'

'You have a scrapbook'

'Scrapbook?'

'You can force others to write stuff about you and chat with you.'

'Oh'

'People with lot of scraps are treated with respect in our groups.'

'I want to try this out. Please help me create a login in Orkut.'

'Sure. And you can do all kind of activities if you can make friends with many in Orkut.'

'How do you make friends in Orkut? I eagerly want to check the photos of Clara, that bio tech girl, about whom all our college guys were talking about during the induction program.'

'You must send them a friend request and if they accept your request, you guys will become friends and then you can check whatever she puts up and vice versa.'

'Can't the girls give me a friend request?'

'They can. But they won't.'

'Why is that?'

'Ego'

'Oh. What is the best option to make friends?'

'There will be lot of random users who would accept your friend request, simply because they would want to have a huge friend list. Send them a request, they will add you.'

'I will do that. Have you ever loved, Justin?' Chris deviated from the topic.

'No man. Why do you ask me?'

'No. I just wanted to know.'

'But I always wanted to.' We reached our apartment. Chris initially visited us occasionally in my place for chatting and playing play station games with me, until one day when my mother served him food. From that certain day, he made sure that he was present in my house during breakfast, lunch and dinner. 'I created a book with all the factors that a girl needs to satisfy to fall in love with me.'

'Ha, in this world where you found it tough to get a girl for the past 17 years, you have created a book that has factors that a girl needs to satisfy to get into your book! That's funny. Where is that book?'

'In my head'

'Hmmm . . . Some book you have created, I must say. Anyways, what are the factors that a girl needs to satisfy, to get into your book?'

'They should have noticeable assets!' Before the start of college, I trimmed my hair and sported a French beard. I wore oval shaped spectacles to suit my long face.

'You mean wealth and property? That's surprising. I thought you were the one who did not go behind money.'

'Chris, assets means good looks, bright smile etc. Everything which makes her special'

'Okay, got it.'

'They should be talkative!'

'You want them to be talkative so you can speak with them all night?'

'No. Because I am talkative and only a person with the same character understands the other better.' People called me a *scholar* because I sounded more theoretical than imaginary when I spoke. But there were other gangs of guys calling me different names. Some called me *squeaky toy*, some *psych*, but majority stuck to *scholar*.

'No wonder people call you squeaky toy.' Chris chuckled. 'Next?'

'They should be mallus.'

'And anything else?'

'Above all, they should be intelligent! I don't intend to work after 30.'

'Ah! You will complete your college at the age of 21 and most probably by 22 you will start working. And you will quit work at the age of 30?'

'Exactly'

'Just 8 years of work? That's it?'

'If you look at it as 8 years, it is just 8 years. But if you look at it as 2920 days, which is equal to 70080 hours, which is in turn equal to 4204800 minutes of hardship, man it is tough.'

'Now that's scary.'

'I told you.'

'Why should the girl be mallu?' Chris smiled. 'Comes from your roots, does it?'

'No. I missed out on Namitha, my 12th grade physics tuition mate. She was a bomb and a mallu but I lost her to a Gujju!' I felt sad. 'But I should say that was a good starting point.'

'You just told me that you wanted to love. But as per what you said, isn't Namitha your 1st love?'

'I lost her because I had never spoken with her.'

'Hmmm . . . you kept staring at her I suppose.'

'She came with her boyfriend to tuition every day.'

'That means you were trying for a fish that was already caught.' Chris chuckled. 'How did you get the name *psych*? I always wanted to ask you, because that's how those kids who come to play football call you.'

'Oh that? I predicted Arsenal's victory against Leeds united in the 2003 FA cup.'

'Wasn't that the time when Arsenal as a unit was expected to win the match against a weakened Leeds united squad?'

'Yes. Sadly those guys did not know that Arsenal was playing in the premier league. And I won't complain because they were outdated with respect to the information they had.'

'I'll accept that. They were not even aware of the fact that the babe in the daily soap about lifeguards and beaches did not own those huge boobs anymore. I noticed that when I joined you for a match of football with them a week back.'

'You mean she has removed all the silicon? Sorry, but I am outdated too, with respect to this case.'

'Are you boys having dinner?' my mom asked.

'I was waiting for it.' Chris was crazy about food (especially the food served by my mom) and with the clock striking 8 'o clock, his stomach took control over him. 'I am coming!' We immediately took the seat next to my aging father at the dining table

'I thought your grandmother has prepared dinner for you?' My dad asked Chris.

'I wouldn't dare touch it. It will taste as bad as her age.' Chris chuckled.

'Your grandmother won't like that. So tell me about your first day in college.' My father asked.

'Let me start!' Chris started. 'The class is filled with contrasting characters, as per what we deduced after interacting with two of our classmates.' He ate quickly. 'One was a movie enthusiast, Param. He keeps talking about movies and movies alone. Man, for a day he spoke so much. And the other was this guy called Nithin. He was numb the entire day.'

'And what do you have to say about the college facilities and rules?'

'Facilities are fine. Rules are bad.'

'Which means you guys had a bad time in college today, I assume.'

'That's called insult in my books, dad.' I said as Chris dug into his plate. 'We are smart, intelligent and guys with integrity. There are none like us in the class!' I exclaimed.

'Yeah' Chris agreed. 'The director of our college came up to us, and gave us some exclusive advice, during the induction program. All of them looked at us with respect.'

'I heard about the kind of respect you guys got. The two of you were the only idiots who did not wear ties!'

'Jones's father informed your daddy about it, honey.' My mother, kept a plate of fried chicken in front of us. 'And he sounded really happy about it.'

'That Jones's ass' I whispered to myself.

'I don't care a damn about what they have to say. You know that, Justin.' My dad said. 'But it is insulting to know that you didn't follow the rules in the very first day of your college life.'

'Guess we are one of a kind in that class' Chris chuckled.

'You had your dinner didn't you?' My father was not impressed. 'Go back home and sleep.' He ordered.

'I was thinking of trying out the chicken placed here.' Chris said politely. 'It will take me another 20 minutes, uncle.'

'For the quantity of food you consume here, I think we are permitted to charge you.' My father replied.

'Why is that uncle? I thought aunty loves cooking food for me.'

'She used to.' My father informed 'But with you easily consuming as much as the three of us do, I am not very pleased.'

'Guests are the human form of God on earth, uncle.' Chris replied.

'Not when the guest raids through the resources of the inmates . . .' And the argument rallied on.

*　　*　　*

'Isn't Jeffrey your schoolmate?' Chris asked me.

'You already know about Jeffrey and me.' I reminded him.

'I know that.' Chris said. 'But I noticed that you tried talking to him twice. Why did you even try to talk with him in the first place when you know he won't reply?'

'Simple. We think differently.' I answered.

'Elaborate.'

'Take my schoolmate Vicky for example. When I was in good terms with Jeffrey in 10th grade, I looked upon Vicky with respect. Jeffrey told me he doesn't like Vicky.'

'Who is Vicky?' Chris asked.

'He is a rich kid.'

'And why doesn't Jeffrey like him?'

'He is gay.'

'Ah!' Chris smiled. 'He tried to bang Jeffrey?'

'No. People say Jeffrey tried to patch up with him and Vicky disagreed.'

'That sounds dumb and taking into consideration that Jeffrey was attracted to Divya, that girl who was seated in the front row of our classroom, I am sure the people who blamed Jeffrey can go and suck each other's dicks.' Chris roared.

'What if those people were girls?'

'What if those people were girls?'

'At the end of the day, Jeffrey hates a lot of people: Black and White.' Hoping Chris would believe me 'You'll come to learn more as time goes by.' I assured Chris.

'He fought with you and hates you for a dumb reason, accepted, but that might not be the same reason why he hates everyone! He might have had really bad experience with others too. You never know'

'Frodo believed Gollum.'

'In the end Gollum was not that bad!'

'Let gays be gays.' I laughed, assuming I cracked a joke. 'Let's get back to business. 17 years in Bangalore and now in Chennai. New city, new people, and just one friend in me, whom you know only for the past 60 days. You think you can manage here, now that we will have to spend almost half a day every weekday in that college for the next four years?'

'Want to bet?'

'Ah! I am here to help you.'

'I know.' His mobile rang and he quickly put it on silent mode.

'Who is that in the call?' I asked Chris as he walked off. 'You always walk off from the scene whenever a call comes. Are you hiding something or "someone" from me?'

'No . . .' Chris said. 'Go sleep.'

Chapter 4

English Matters

'It's 8'o clock. Get in.' we were standing at the corridor, just outside our college classroom, when the block in charge stood tall.

'Who the fuck is he to impose rules on us?' I asked Chris, as I reluctantly got into the class with the rest of the students.

'He is the *block in-charge.*' Chris informed.

'I know that. Why the hell should we listen to some random idiot?'

'If you are not aware about who block in charges are, then here are the facts. Block in-charges are traditionally jobless thugs hired by the college officials to control and maintain discipline among students and staffs alike. Anyone indulging in mischievous activities will have to face the wrath of the block in charge. They are authorized to even to throw any student or staff out of this college.' Chris told loudly as we took our seats in the last row.

Traditionally people who came in late to classes were forced to take the first bench seats in schools and colleges. But in my college it was different. Girls were forced to occupy the seats in the 1st three rows and boys from the 4th row. So all the boys immediately caught places behind the girls, keeping the last few rows available for late comers.

'Lucky to have friends who don't fight for the last row' Chris said proudly.

'Thank the girls.' I smiled.

It was over four weeks since classes started and we were part of a unique class with different characteristics.

'People have different characters cause it has more to do with the regions that they come from.' Chris informed me.

'The whole world knows that.' I stated. 'But I would say it is a blessing in disguise, because we learn to interact and live with varied people from various cultural backgrounds at a very young age.'

'How does that help us?'

'It helps us in the long run as we learn to change ourselves based on the situation formed around us, as the world is flooded with thousands of different cultures. Indians are exposed to varied cultural people in their country helping them to interact with people in other countries with ease.'

'Indians learn red tape too.' Chris stated quickly. 'Red tape and corruption are household terms in India.'

'Indians are like supermen who are not affected by kryptonite!' I smiled. 'But sadly they are weakened by every Lois Lane!'

'Do you guys mind explaining why you prefer not to concentrate in my class?' There was a professor taking class, and Chris and I had just realized that. 'I can see that you guys are playing a part in distracting the whole class. I have been observing you two for over 30 minutes.

You have been chatting incessantly. What's going on out there?'

He had a point. Chris and I were disturbing the rest of the class that was simply pretending like they were listening to him.

'Did we actually converse for over 30 minutes?' Chris was surprised, as we stood up reluctantly. 'Man, time travels like a jet train!'

'I agree.' Jeffrey shouted. 'I could hardly listen to you sir and I just couldn't concentrate to what you have been teaching. My parents paid the fees for me to study here, not to be disturbed by such talkative classmates.'

'Welcome mate.' I said as the whole class arose to witness the scene that was shaping up. Jeffrey was one of the few boys who had caught the seat in the 4th row behind the girls. 'Was expecting you to tell something against me, mate.'

'Call me foe.'

'Whatever. You need to concentrate on what he teaches and not with chat with Divya if you want to score high.' I whispered into Jeffrey's ears as I walked towards the staff with Chris.

'How good is she as a friend?' Chris asked Jeffrey.

'Not impressive.'

'Ah ok.' Chris said sadly.

'Shut up you two.' The staff roared.

'Hmmm . . . I am sorry sir.'

'I asked. What was the chit-chat about?' He shouted.

'Nothing serious, sir, I can assure you that.'

'Egoistic kid' Alvin, our professor scoffed. 'And you mind telling me what session I was taking?'

'We would if we knew.' Chris answered bravely.

'Get out.' The professor roared. 'And don't dare get into my class again.'

Chris happily stepped out and pulled me with him. 'He could have told us what class he was taking; at least it would've helped us miss his subsequent sessions.'

I laughed. 'And there I was imaging you to be a soft spoken person.'

'I am to those who I hardly know.'

'Neo also had a pathetic life before Morpheus met him in the matrix.' I informed Chris.

'Why are these Hollywood directors in a compulsion to cast a black as one of the main characters in all the movies they take?' Chris asked me, as we stood next to the class's entrance.

'If they do not do that, they will be called racists.'

'Hmmm . . . It will not be long before a black actually becomes the president of America.'

'Accepted'

'When is the *patcult* interview's scheduled for?'

'Raman informed me that it is scheduled for this coming month end.' I replied.

'Today is the last day of the month my friend.'

'Hmmm . . . then I guess the interviews will take place anytime from now.'

'I salute your optimism. But it actually does not hurt to be pessimistic at times. Remember what you told me a few weeks back?'

'What did I tell you?'

'Even if we do not make it to the initial list, we can eventually make it by winning in some competitions.'

'So you mean to say that they had not planned to have interviews at the first place?'

'They have never conducted interviews from the time the committee was formed. People liked by staffs and known to existing members are always selected.' I stated. 'Param informed.'

'So you mean to say Raman lied?'

'He will make you wait for the next four years!'

'Corruption' I stated.

'Starts at home' Chris completed, as the class ended and everyone left the classroom for tea, except for a set of guys including Jeffrey, who stayed back cause they seemed like they were busy discussing about something I was sure was not worth discussing at all.

One dark guy with thick spectacles also decided to stay back.

'He is Arun Sukumar.' I whispered to Chris. 'You must hear him converse with our class mates.'

'*You asking me to listening to him converge?*' Chris imitated Arun.

'*Ejactly*' I imitated Arun and laughed out, until Arun moved close to us.

'Hi my name is called Arun Sukumar?' Arun stopped Jeffrey and stated. He was born and brought up in Salem and was new to Chennai. He was basically from a merchant family and had his schooling in Salem, where staffs conversed in "Tamil" in English medium classes!

'*We knowing your name all calling Arun Sukumar?* Where did you pick your English from?' Jeffrey could not control his tongue and laughed out loud. 'Oh my god! I am seeing things. Even E.T spoke better than you.'

"A character developed by Herbert's has to be bad in grammar. Period" I thought and agreed. Honestly that is the case with a million Indians graduating from India.

'You guys doing lot of insulting me' Arun Sukumar felt insulted as the Jeffrey and his gang laughed out loud.

'You guys speak no better than him.' I moved across and interfered.

'Here comes Shakespeare.' Jeffrey roared. Arun quickly moved out to the extreme end of the scene as the gang's focus shifted towards me. 'Purify our English, oh great one!'

'Good one, Jeffrey.' Jerome Singh was from Trichy and was Jeffrey's bench mate in class. He wanted to be recognized in class and wanted a taste of city life and Jeffrey promised him that.

'Support eh?'

'Be sportive, bro. if someone teases someone, laugh out loud or leave the scene.' Jerome said.

'Ok, Gen.Thade.'

Jerome was furious, as Arun, Chris and I roared in laughter.

'I thought you will laugh with us?' I asked Jeffrey.

'Fuck you!' Jeffrey replied, as he moved quickly with his group out of the scene.

'Jerome is like Harley Quinn! Behind the Joker to get a slice of city life, promised in a platter!'

'By the way, what does the city life have to offer Jerome that Jeffrey might help him get?'

'Take pictures around the city with varied people to post in Orkut.'

'Ah!' Chris said.

'I think we will find it tough to make friends out here.' I stated sarcastically to Chris. 'I think we must be content with "loving people from Salem who is going to coming for helping us?"'

'That is *come for helping us.*' Arun quickly returned back to scene.

'Whoa! Thanks for correcting me.' I grinned, not sure if he actually corrected me or made another grammatical error.

'Coming for tea?' Arun asked us.

'You carry forward. We have some work here.' I politely replied. Arun smiled and left.

'What work do we have here?' Chris asked.

'To be away from Arun!' I chuckled.

'I respect the chap because it is not his mistake that he is not able to converse in English. It is an issue that should be addressed by the education ministry seriously.

A lot of students studying in English medium don't know to write the word *grammar* correctly!' Chris said.

'No wonder novel sales are yet to touch over the roof numbers.' I replied sadly. 'English is the best medium for networking in the country, though Hindi is our national language. I hope time brings English to schools in rural areas with it! A person good in English is always confident and competent. And once the whole country starts conversing fluently in English, no one stop the countrymen from reaching great heights.' I said. 'Maybe we must play our part in the near future to help people converse in English in villages.'

'I don't care about anything as long as we have each other.' Chris said.

'Now why did you say that?'

'Just thought it was a good line to be added here'

'If that line came out from a girl's mouth, I would have jumped in joy. But coming out from you scares me.' I said. 'That's a dislike.'

'But how do you intend to bring English to the rural population?'

'Simple' I paused.

'Continue' Chris stated.

'We will be supported by banks to construct schools and colleges in rural areas, after successfully attaining high grades in our under graduation.'

'Hmmm . . .' Chris looked insulted. 'By the way things are going, I think we must try and get into the classroom first and foremost about having a successful college life, simply cause if we do not complete our under graduation successfully, all our plans about helping villagers to converse in English, will be washed off with water. And for your kind information this is the third professor, out of the five professors taking classes for us this semester, who has apparently banned us from attending his sessions.'

*   *   *

<u>*October 2005:*</u>

'Good morning, sir.' Chris and I finally got an opportunity to meet Prof. Kern, who headed "patcult".

'Good morning.' Kern hardly weighed 60 and was hardly 5 feet 5 inches. He looked innocent in looks and covered that with a harsh voice and a staunch look. 'Get to the point.'

'Sir I am Justin and this is Chris. We are first year students in the CSE department.' I replied.

'Get to the point please.'

'Sir we would like you to put some light in the patcult initiative and let us know how we can get into this committee.'

'Hmmm . . . you guys can come back next year to know about patcult. Cause the college officials have strictly disapproved 1st years from joining this committee.'

'So will there be an interview held up next year for us?'

'Yes interviews will take place. But majority of them are selected based on the talent they showcase during the annual intra college competitions that will be conducted in the 1st week of January.'

'Oh!'

'And those who do not win will have to prove themselves in inter college competitions, that will be conducted extensively all around the nation.'

'When will the registrations start for the intra college competitions sir?'

'As soon as 1st semester exams are up.' He smiled. 'Justin is your name right?'

'Right, sir'

'So Justin, do well in the competitions in January, which will help you will make it easily to the list. Those who excelled in the intra-college events usually ended up heading various committees here. Those who do not make it to the list, usually end up as spectators.'

'During the induction program, they informed us that those who lose in 3 consecutive events will be chucked out of the committee. Does that happen?'

'We can't afford to change the committee on a periodic basis. To maintain stability, people who get into the committee, remain in the committee.'

* * *

December 2005:

'I don't understand.' Chris stated as the list of events to be conducted during the annual intra-college competitions, named _Sansar,_ was issued. 'The list is out with the names of the participants in it?'

'Hmmm . . .' Deepakh started. 'Guess that's called politics.' Deepakh was our college bench mate and eventually a new inductee into our club (tentatively titled "Door Squad"), simply because he regularly served time outside the class as much as we did. He was 170cms in height and was well built at 70 kgs. He had oval spectacles and was fair in color. He had no facial hair, and was generally talkative in nature.

'And sadly the only event open in _lece,_ an event in which the person should race with his competitors, with a lemon in a spoon in his mouth, for 20 meters. And the winner gets to keep the spoon and the lemon!' Chris informed.

'Ah! Some sort of gift to look out for.' I roared in anger. 'How could they do it to us?'

'Do what to us?' Chris asked.

'Not give us an opportunity to participate in these events.'

'Look at the people who have made it to the list. For dance it is Jeffrey and Jones. For light music it is Jerome and Jackie. For debate it is Joshua. For dramatics it is Jero, Jeffrey and John. Bloody everyone's name is starting with J. The only person whose name starts with J but has not made it to the list is you Justin.' Deepakh informed. 'There were 8 slots available for 1st year boys, for the competitions, and it has all gone to the *terror gang!*' Jeffrey and his group called themselves as the terror guys, because they imagined themselves as people who terrorized the normal crowd by their sheer presence. 'Terror gang! Fuckers were supported by that bloody asshole.'

'Who, Jeremiah?'

'Yes, that same fucker! He is Jeffrey's 1st cousin and has been helping him in all kind of shitty things, like making friends with block in-charges, getting acquainted with staffs and various other stuff. Man if not for him, Jeffrey would have not been present even in the attendance sheet.'

'And above all, Professor Kern stated that no 1st years will be allowed to join the club. Ass conducted the interview in the end when Raman informed where guys interviewed were 8 and all 8 made it.' Chris added

'Leave it dude. Anyways, Jeffrey is not a great stage artist. I know about that guy. He peed on stage when we participated in a cultural competition some time back. He will never perform well on stage.' I assured him. 'But it is sad that assholes like him will be able to get into the coveted committee before we do.' I stated.

'No wonder family politics prevail in our nation. First father, then daughter, then son, then son's wife and now there are talks that the great grandson has not tied the knot because he is targeting the coveted prime minister post.' Chris informed.

Chapter 5

Instincts

As semesters went by all the professors, except Alvin, allowed us to attend their sessions. And with we shifted from Orkut to Facebook.

'You checked out what's coming up?' I asked Chris.

'LSN College is conducting their annual cultural program!' He answered.

'Wow! Isn't that great news?' I was excited.

'But are we allowed to participate there?' Chris asked me pessimistically. 'As in, will the donkeys who are part of the patcult committee allow us to go there?'

'Hmmm . . .' I thought silently for a minute with Chris. Jeffrey did not participate in the events that took place in January this year, because he was down due to some unknown disease. Only I knew that it was actually a phobia called stage fright, which was the subset of gloss phobia. But thanks to Jeremiah, he got into the committee with ease and took over the representative post for our batch, and his co-members compromised of his terror gang.

The only exception in the committee was Raman, a senior jackass, who spent most of his time in the CSE department typing letters and sending mails to people all over the world. In simple terms, he was the CSE department HOD's pet, who recommended him to the committee. And not surprisingly, Raman's task in the committee was to type mails and letters and prepares lists for various competitions. 'What do you think?'

'Let's wait and see.' I told Chris. 'But this does sound interesting.' I smiled. 'Heard cultural programs are organized really well in LSN College, which is tentatively titled as Instincts.'

'Cool' Deepakh joined the discussion. He spent most of the time with us and despised Jeffrey and his group. I expected the guys and girls in my class to actually hate the terror gang, because they were simply the most irritating group that I had ever come across in my life.

They walked up and down the stairs during the tea break, again and again, simply because they felt it was cool to move up and down the steps for no reason. They even stood outside the toilet, and stared hard at anyone who went in to answer nature's call. This was done frequently because someone misguided them into believing that standing outside the toilet and staring at people invoked fear in the concerned person.

But surprisingly people in my class supported them as everyone felt licking the slippers of these idiots will help them bag OD (On Duty) for upcoming cultural competitions (The committee members had rights to prepare the list with any person they want in it). When classes started, almost everyone in class felt participating in cultural competitions was actually a waste of time, but as days went by the idea of winning hit everyone. And that reflected in majority of the student's marks, as the eligibility for participating for competitions was 65% minimum in all the semesters and everyone scored above 70%.

'LSN College is also the hunting ground for girls. And compared to school cultural programs, it is totally different.'

'Taking into consideration the things that you told me a few months back, can I consider it as the place where girls don't put artificial boobs and come for the program, right?' Chris asked me.

'Shit dude, not that. I am referring to the fact that the participants do their homework for the show and use tricks to win on stage.' I smiled.

'But the bad news is that Raman has been given the responsibility of selecting the participants for the various events in LSN College.' Deepakh said quickly. 'I don't think he will take us in.' he said. 'And I hate him.'

'Why do everyone LIKE that fucker in the CSE department?' Chris asked.

'It's not because they want to like him, but only because all the staffs are forced to like him.' Deepakh replied.

'I read in the recent edition of the department magazine that Raman helped Mrs. Meena, our networking staff, in completing her paper for her thesis. It seems he worked day and night with her.' I stated.

'I read that. But you know what? Her thesis was initially rejected by the Madras University, but was later accepted after University reevaluated it and accepted it!' Deepakh added.

'Oh . . . what went wrong?' Chris asked.

'It had Raman's name as the watermark.' Deepakh chuckled.

'And they still like him?' Chris asked.

'Hmmm . . . he used his contacts to help the HOD complete her thesis.' I said.

Other than patcult and exams, the only other talking point in our class was about our department's dearest girl child, Divya, who came forward and started a brawl here.

'You know I tried getting Divya's number and finally when I got her number, she disconnected her mobile and left the college.' Chris murmured. 'Dude, people say she was pregnant and that was why she left college.'

'What? That's bullshit, Chris.' I shouted.

'But she vomited daily.' Chris defended himself

Both Jeffrey and Dhinesh loved her and they were the only two guys who had her mobile number. But I heard one of them forwarded her mobile number to some person who disturbed her all night. Dhinesh was the son of a babuji and he dealt in millions with everyone. It was surprising to know that he feel for Divya, a girl from a mediocre Brahmin family, who was neither beautiful nor rich. Jeffrey loved her simply because she was the only fair girl in my class (Tamil Brahmins are generally fair in complexion).

'These assholes, Jeffrey and Dhinesh, who officially fell for her, must have not seen the world.' Deepakh stated. 'Cause any day girls much prettier and sexier are found in abundance in the world, but sadly God dumped the ugly ones in our college and specifically in our class.'

Jerome and Jeffrey supported Divya. *We will help you find the person* they promised her, while Dhinesh and some others were against her. Intentionally or unintentionally, I got involved in this issue and the end result was *All's bad that started bad*

Boys were connected with Girls via sign language. They communicated over the phone lines all night and tried to make a life with them. Surprisingly the amount spent for buying a mobile, and paying for recharging the same touched close to 3000s for them.

'I know why she used to vomit daily. She was suffering from food poisoning!' I informed Chris and Deepakh.

'Oh. How do you know that?' Chris asked me.

'I let her have a bite of my sandwich.' I said hesitantly.

'Oh! You have never let me have a bite of your sandwich. Man, don't tell me you are the fox who made the right moves.'

'No dude. The sandwich was spoilt and I wanted to dispose it, but seeing Divya had already vomited everything she consumed, I thought she could have it.' I smiled

'That's cheap. So people screwed you up because you let her have a bite of your spoilt sandwich?' Deepakh asked. 'No one told me this.' He said sadly. 'Actually no one tells me anything!'

'All of them wanted a bite of my spoilt sandwich!' I smirked. 'Which no one got. One of them stated that *bringing food was a crime in our college which you have already committed and letting a girl have a bite is a bigger crime.*'

'Who told you that?' Deepakh asked.

'Jeffrey' I replied politely.

'And all of them hate you for that?' Chris asked me.

'Yes' I smiled. 'But luckily he did not inform the block-in-charges about it. He does have a heart I guess.'

'Lucky he has. Cause if he would have, the block-in-charges would have ensured you never ate anything after that.' Chris chuckled. 'Now I understand why our class mates do not consume anything that you secretly bring from home.'

'All for a spoilt sandwich' I said.

'Sad that she left dude. She was a good girl.' Chris sympathized her.

'Ah! That's touching. You like her?' I asked Chris.

'That is wrong!' Chris said. 'I am not some Prince in some journey with a tooth tied as a locket to his chain, who has no other choice but to marry a girl kept in a castle for a lot of fucking years.'

'One year.' I stopped him.

'Thanks for correcting me.' He smiled. 'God knows what the witches and medusas did to her.'

'Are you referring to some real time character?' Deepakh asked him.

'Naaa . . . this is from an author's book asked me to specifically mention this line, so that people will get curious and read it.' Chris said.

'That's heights of dumbness. Almost all the books, movies and serials have witches, wizards and medusas.' I stated.

'The author is Prithvin Ramendran, a second year student in LSN College, who is aggressively pushing his book.' Chris informed.

'LSN College? Will he help us win something there, if we get to participate there?' Deepakh asked.

'I think he might if we buy a copy of his book.' Chris chuckled, as Deepakh and I grinned.

'Right, that's a fair deal.' Deepakh said. 'Ok, on a serious note, you think abortion is wrong, especially when it concerns an 18 year old girl?' Deepakh asked us.

'Yes, when you look at it as killing a "to be born baby" who has not done anything wrong but will die for no mistake of his/her, it is wrong. But when a young girl has to face this bloody society and answer all sorts of questions, for which she will have no answer for, we have a case.' I replied.

'You may be right!' Chris grinned.

Divya left the college, after which Jeffrey became a close friend of Dhinesh.

'Dhinesh's father is organizing a workshop next week. They are expecting a lot of people to attend that.'

'What is the workshop about?'

'*Love and be loved for free.*'

'Don't you think we must go and have a word with Raman?' Chris asked

'About what?' I asked him.

'For getting our names registered in the list of students who will be given OD for attending the cultural program to be conducted in LSN College?' Chris answered politely.

'I don't think it's a "cup of tea." 'Deepakh replied.

'Then "what" is like a cup of tea?' Chris asked.

'Hmmm . . . Cappuccino?' Deepakh replied.

'Cappuccino is a type of coffee idiot.' I informed.

'I was kidding . . .' Deepakh surrendered.

'Let's give it a shot!' I said. 'I heard they have dumb charades in the long list of events. And I am good at it and I am sure no one else will enroll for that. And above all, every college can enroll close to 10 teams for the event.'

'Wait!' Chris acted as if he was removing his dress. 'Try me.'

'Titanic?'

'Man, you are seriously good.' Chris said. 'But how did you find that out?'

'Cause that is the only scene I remember in that flick.' I said proudly. 'Actually that is the only scene Indians would remember from that movie!'

'And people say it is a masterpiece!' Chris said. 'We are seriously perverts.'

'Hmmm . . .' I thought. 'We must surely not miss this opportunity. LSN will be a good start to our competitive career. And maybe I can find a girl there worthy of being included in my book.'

'I have not seen your book, though you mention it all the time. May I see it once?' Deepakh asked.

'It is in his head!' Chris interfered.

'Oh . . .'

*   *   *

'Can you include our name in that list? We are anyway "out-standing" in majority of the classes and have a lot of time to burn.' I walked across to Raman and asked.

'The list is complete!' Raman shouted, at me and the rest of the class. 'For those who did not make it to the list, better luck next time.'

'May I at least see the event list?' I asked Raman.

'Sure.' Raman said. 'And you know the college will give you OD if you come back with a winning certificate.'

'Thanks for the info.' I smiled.

'My pleasure' He gave the list and walked out. 'Keep the list in my table. I am going out.'

'There you have it.' I turned back and said to Chris and Deepakh. 'You think that next time will ever come?'

'If *next time* comes out from an Indian's mouth, it will be a *no*.' Deepakh looked defeated.

'Accepted! That bastard had the list ready even before the OD form was issued, as I said.' I said. 'I am sure about that.'

*   *   *

'We are selecting people who are potential winners!' Jeffrey's group comprised of Jerome and Jones. 'Cause it is better to be with winners than wannabes!'

'I am a proven winner.' I informed Jeffrey. 'Heard you can rework the list, if you want to'

'You think so bro?' Jeffrey queried me. 'College and school are different. You will see.'

'Ok. Why wouldn't you say that? You never ever won in any event in school.' I replied quickly. 'The whole world knows what you did on stage with me in school.'

'What the fuck did he do?' Chris asked me, teasing Jeffrey.

'Mind your words, Justin.' Jeffrey intervened. 'Tell me, how many did you win?'

'One'

'I remember that. You bagged the third place in the painting competition during the annual school cultural competition when we were in the 12th grade. And I was not surprised because there were only three participants.'

I did not reply and turned to Chris. 'So that leaves me with you and Deepakh, to bunk and give a shot on stage there!'

'What a team.' Jerome chuckled.

'We will win.' Chris said confidently. 'By the way, what are you talking about?'

'I am referring to the three of us bunking college and attending the events in the cultural program in LSN College.'

'Oh.' Deepakh said. 'I would love to, but I am actually held up this coming month with assignments and project work.'

'We don't have any project work.' I stated, as Jeffrey and his gang giggled. Deepakh was an outstanding student in class, not because he stood with us outside the class room, but also because he was the topper in the department.

'But we might. I am preparing for the 4th year project.' Deepakh stated.

'The majority of the events conducted there need at least 3 individuals in each team, to call it a team and enroll themselves.' I explained to Deepakh. 'Provided Chris or I have a twin we did not know for so long, who turns up on that day and makes our "team" a team.' I explained. 'That's 99% not possible.' I said with disgust. 'But it also says that the three need not be from the same College. But we would love to have you as our third team member.'

'Are you referring to dumb charades?' Deepakh asked. 'Don't they have events like quiz and debugging? I think two will do for those events.'

'No. Those events require us using the brain, like quiz.' I stated.

'Hmmm . . . like asking Homer Simpson to solve a bloody mathematics problem?' Chris added.

'Good you got it right.' I smiled.

'You fuckers sit and plan out what to do there, while we go and get our OD for the events.' Jeffrey stopped our conversation. 'But I would recommend you guys to sit tight in your respective places and count the stars up in the sky. There is no need for you guys to try out things that you guys might not be good at.' He paused for a moment, as others smiled. 'But I would love to see you lose where I win.' He whispered in my ear. 'I want to show why I am better than you.'

'Keep dreaming.'

'I will.' He said cunningly. 'Let the world know that Jeffrey Ben Martin was any day better than Justin Zachariah. I proved it by beating you to becoming the head of patcult initiative and now I will beat you on stage to.'

'Let's go.' I pulled Chris and Deepakh and left the place. 'I am not wasting time with these idiots.'

The guys behind Jeffrey stepped forward to hit me, only to be pulled back by Jeffrey. 'Don't hit the kid. He will die.' They roared in laughter.

He was actually right. Jero, Joshua and Jerome were all well-built and one blow from either of them might have been enough for me to get a room in a "bone and joint hospital", for I was too weak to compete against the big guns of *the terror gang*. But I actually did not mind that because I badly needed a break from college and a medical leave would have been good enough for me to get a solid week off.

Surprisingly, except CSE department the rest of the departments were not interested in sending their students for cultural. Therefore the HOD of the CSE department automatically became the chairman of the patcult committee, replacing Kern, which in turn gave all the CSE students an opportunity to participate in the event. All expect us!

'That bastard Jeffrey and his gang will be absent for a week.' I said in disgust.

'One whole week? I thought the program in LSN College runs for two days.' Chris stated as Deepakh left with Arun Sukumar to the laboratory.

'His team gets five days preparation time.' I said.

'So what are they going to participate in?' Chris said. 'Western dance and light music, I heard.'

'Yes. I would like to see Jeffrey dance.' I said. 'He has been cheating the world by promising a performance on stage, but has never done so.'

'Ha . . . Coward!'

'I know why you would love to see him dance. He learnt his dance moves from Mr. Bean.' I giggled.

'Hmmm . . . So are we going or not? I wouldn't mind bunking a day, as you said, not only because I am sure we might find someone there and win, but mainly to see these losers lose.'

'If you insist' I smiled. 'Who knows? Our twin might turn up.' I thought for a moment. 'We must definitely go. And you know what, I know just the person whom I can convince to join us.'

I did not like the idea of having a girl as a team mate. The other groups in the class were most interested in making friends with girls by taking them into their teams.

They add flavor to our participation. They'd say. *Assholes!* I thought.

'Tomorrow we might actually have a girl in our team and she could bring be the difference.' Chris said optimistically.

'I am not buying that.' I did not agree.

'Tomorrow we might have a team mate who is actually from the opposite sex!' Chris sounded like a future teller.

'That's the second time in as many dialogues that you have told me that. Never in a team which includes me will there be a girl.' I informed.

'We will see about that!'

When people were busy making groups for the cultural events, my class was already boasting about the different groups that had been formed over the past one year, apart from the terror gang. One group with movie enthusiasts headed by Param, an evangelist group headed by Chacko and Rahul, another group filled with cricket crazy fans headed by Ganesh and the remaining fell into a group dedicated to sleeping. And every group, except the sleeping gang, was an ally to the terror gang.

'I heard that Jerome asshole call us *the piles group.'* Chris said sadly.

'Fucker, why does he call us that?' I was very angry to hear that.

'Simply because we never sit in class!' Chris stated. 'So he does have a point.'

'We must call ourselves the *cult gurus.* People ready to take the cultural circle by storm.'

'Hmmm . . . we waited a whole year, trying nothing and waiting for a call from Patcult, which never happened and will most probably not happen too.' Chris said. He was right. This was one of the many cultural events which popped up but sadly we played the waiting game. 'If we win our name will have some value, or else it will have no relevance to us.'

'I know.' I thought for a moment and continued. 'But believe me: the wait will be worth it.'

'One minute' Chris told me, as he took out his mobile and moved out of the scene.

'Do they have any competition on mathematic problems?' Ranbir asked. He was mad about Mathematics and was credited for starting the mathematics department in our college that helped people solve mathematic problems with ease. And believe me, it helped a lot.

'No. This is a cultural program. They will only have events like Indian music, western music, dramatics, ad-zap, dance etc.'

'Sad. Someone must take an initiative to include creative competitions which will help us learn while having fun.' He said quickly.

'Hmmm . . . That's a fucked up idea.'

*   *   *

The day started at 4:00 am next day. It was one of the most important days of my life.

Finally, I was going to set foot in another college for a cultural program. The clock ticked slowly.

I thought about checking out some porn flicks and switched on my personal desktop, only to be interrupted by a call.

'Hello.' A voice said. 'How are you and what are you doing?'

'Nothing' I replied 'I am fine'

'Can I be a part of your team?'

'Team? We don't have a team or anything as such.' I said.

'You asked me yesterday night if I am available for the day and my answer is yes.'

'I knew the answer will be yes the moment I got the call. Make sure you are there and stay there with your mouth shut.'

I did not get a reply.

'You can talk now.'

'Ok.'

'Cool.'

'See you in a while.'

Immediately after cutting the call, I dialed one of the only few numbers I memorized, that of Chris. His number was engaged.

'What the fuck is he doing at this time of the day?' I said to myself. *Deepakh told me only guys who have girlfriends are engaged in the phone lines 24 hours of the day.*

I cut the call and dialed Chris' number again after 15 minutes, which was now free. I was not prepared to quiz him early in the morning. 'You know, I got a call from an ass this morning, stating he wants to be a part of our team.' I informed Chris.

'That's gay!' he replied. He was half asleep as I explained about the call I received.

'Yeah he calls himself *Rejo*. That sounds gay too.' I replied.

'You interested in including him in our team?' Chris asked me seriously.

'You never know, it might be worth it!' I said thoughtfully. 'He was part of my plan, as in was the only person willing to bunk college and come with us.'

'Oh.'

'God blesses us when we help the weak.'

'Ha ha.' I was sure it was not a joke. 'So how do you intend to go to LSN College? Are you taking your car?' Chris asked casually.

'Are you sponsoring petrol?' I stated.

'No. You are the one who owns a car.' He answered quickly.

'What about the car that's parked in your parking?' I quizzed him.

'That's my grandparents' car. I will never touch it.'

'Why?'

'If we take the car out, Mohan will park his car there.'

'India. Then it will be bus.'

'Bus? I don't usually travel by bus. My parents have always told me to use a car to go anyplace I go.' He forgot that we were travelling everyday to college by bus.

'This whole plan was yours, though it is mine. I'm getting involved in it because you are involved in it, which has forced me into getting involved in it. I will therefore not waste cash from my already thin wallet, as if not for you I would have been sleeping and so . . . .'

'Ok. I did not understand what you just said, but I am pretty sure that you are blabbering and I don't want you to waste your energy for convincing me. So accepted, bus it will be!' Sleep was getting on to him.

'Cool'

'But if anything happens to me, you will be held responsible for it.' Chris warned.

'That doesn't scare me!' I chuckled.

*   *   *

I stood in front of the shower and took a quick bath and got ready for the day.

'Leaving early today?' My father noticed me getting ready. 'Jones' father informed me that he is going to some college for some cultural program.'

'Yes. I am also going to LSN College to participate in their annual cultural program.'

'Hmmm . . . sounds interesting. What's it called?'

'Instincts'

'Nice. So what does your instinct say? Will you win there?'

I will be happy if they allow me to participate there. 'Surely'

'But Jones' father informed me that you were not selected into some cultural committee, simply because you were not talented.' My father stated. 'But his son made it through because they identified him as a rising talent.'

'Bullshit.'

'I know that.' My father laughed. 'All the best'

'Thanks.' I moved towards him. 'It will be better if you add your wishes in my wallet too.'

'I already have.'

I dug into my wallet and found 35rs in it. 'I had Rs. 30 in my wallet yesterday night. And now it is Rs. 35. You added 5 bucks? I never knew you were so cheap, dad.'

'You better leave or else you might be looking at 30 again.'

That is good enough because the travel upwards costs 5 bucks and downwards costs 7 bucks, leaving me with 23 bucks for food. I thought.

The clock struck 7 and it was time to take the bus.

'How much do you have?' Chris came out of his house and we started walking towards the bus stop.

'250 Bucks" Chris said.

'Good. That means my lunch is sponsored today.' I smiled. 'I hope you will do that, because I am sure you would not want to see your friend, who has always been there for you, dying of hunger in some unknown college.'

'Hmmm' Chris said nothing. We stood in the bus stop for over 5 minutes and saw no signs of the local 121A bus which took passengers to that college.

'You sure the bus is coming?' Chris asked me. 'It is 7:15 and the bus should have reached this stop by now. I think we missed it.'

'This is India, Chris. Nothing comes on time, except orgasm' I chuckled. 'Here if the time for the bus is 7:10, you can expect it to reach this place by 7:30. So we are actually 15 minutes early.' I smiled.

'You think there will be many like us who will come to LSN College?'

'We won't find many people of our type there but we will surely find lot of pseudo-intellectual assholes fighting to bag the prizes.'

'Who told you that?'

'Rejo'

'Hmmm . . .'

'I know'

'You know what: my friend told me nowadays lot of chicks travel by bus to such colleges.'

'I am pretty sure many good ones will turn up there in LSN College, but not in such a bus stop.'

'You never know'

'They arrrrrrrrrreeeeeee noooooooottttt . . . .' A car stopped in front of the bus stop and two girls stepped out.

Chapter 6

Shruthi and Preethi

'Looks like you are wrong.' Chris' eyes twinkled.

Hot I said to myself, as the girls waved goodbye to an aging man, probably their father, and stood next to us. One of them stood tall at 172cms and was dressed in a pink t-shirt and blue jeans with trendy canvas Adidas shoes to cover her feet. She was fair and had a pony tail. Her lips were red and her chin was long, but her face was covered by a layer of cream. The other girl was slightly shorter and was dressed in a green round neck t-shirt and a white skirt. She had a short chin and small eyes. *Wow!*

'They are as fair as mallus!' Chris said. 'They are easily going to get into your books.'

'Their father did not have the courtesy to drop them till college. He must be a miser.' I concluded.

'He is spending enough for their cosmetics and clothes. Poor chap must have emptied his pockets on maintaining them.' Chris said sadly. He had a point.

Their clothes and shoes were all branded and it would have cost the poor man a fortune.

'I think we should go and talk to them.' I said boldly.

'In this state?' Chris asked cheekily.

'What do you mean by this state, Chris?'

'What if our little brother reacts when we go closer to them?' Chris looked uneasy. I knew what was running in his mind.

'Ah . . . No wonder my mother asked me to talk and be comfortable around girls. It helps us in situations like these. I now understand how the vampire would have felt when he fell for the blonde and had a torturous love life with her. Guess you are having the same pain.' I stated.

'He poured when he met his love? They never showed that on screen.'

'Forget it.'

'It's has nothing to do with girls. It has to do more with the kind of girls you talk with.'

'I don't get it.' The bus arrived and out of nowhere three more boys turned up and got in first into the bus, followed by Chris and me and finally the two girls got in.

'I think it was *ladies first* that my teacher in school taught me.' Chris informed.

'Lucky the bus is empty, or else you wouldn't even think about it.' I replied. 'And the teacher who told you that must have been a lady, if I am not wrong!'

'Man, you are bang on target. How did you find that out?' Chris was amazed.

'You don't need to know rocket sciences for that, Chris! Women are like that, too predictable.' I said.

'But we never questioned her credibility.'

'That's because a lady is a lady. You don't want to get into the bad books of the women do you?'

'No. Heard the whole country supports and screws up anyone who gets his name enrolled in a woman's book.'

'Right'

'Why don't guys have something like that?'

'I have an answer for that. Men are soft and submissive in nature. They will hand over the book for a smile.' I said sadly.

'Dude I read a certain article which said to win a girl's hand in India, we must first convince her parents. Is that true?'

'Don't tell me you don't know that.' I replied. 'It is not enough for you to love the girl, as in, you must also love her parents and her relatives.'

'What if I don't?'

'Elope'

We sat in the second last row of the bus. I sat in the aisle seat as Chris loved the window seat. Surprisingly, the bus, though was a government bus, was flooded with students who were travelling to LSN College. And not surprisingly, the bus' final stop was LSN College 'The weather is good' Chris stated. 'I feel sleepy.' Chris bought our tickets. I still had my 35 bucks in hand.

I felt sleepy too . . . I woke up rather early and it was only a matter of seconds before my eyes shut.

'Hi.' One of the girls came and woke us up.

'Hi.' I replied with a wide grin.

'What do you have to say about me and my beauty?' She asked me. I sat shocked and so was Chris.

'I am a beauty ignoramus.' I lied.

'You are lying.' She came close to me.

'What are you trying to do?'

'Kiss me.'

'No'

'Yes'

'Am I dreaming?' I asked. 'Pinch me Chris!'

I felt the pain as Chris pinched me and I opened my eyes to the real world. I was disappointed at coming back to reality. 'You were dreaming about something which you can share with me.'

'Shit. Curse me. It was good.' I stared hard at Chris. 'Thanks for waking me up.'

'No issues.' I was dreaming. 'I am always there for you.'

'At all the wrong times' I was upset and sat quietly. 'My dream was better.' I smiled unwillingly. We saw that both the girls had their eyes glued to their mobile phones.

'Hi.' A nerd came to me. Believe me, Chennai, the place where I was born and brought up, is a breeding place for nerds. Every other kid looked ten years over his age, as he is out there to prove that he is better than the nerd sitting next to him. Not only colleges, but also buses were flooded by them.

'Hi.' I wished him back.

'I'm Suresh.' He stretched out his hand towards me.

Chris smiled and whispered low in my ears. 'Wannabe'

'Nice, this is Chris.' Chris smiled. 'And I am Justin.'

'Nice to meet you two' He looked happy to meet us. We were nearing our destination. 'So I assume you guys are also going to participate in the cultural program that is taking place in LSN College.'

'That's right.' I said. 'Just participate.' I smiled. 'And only if they permit' I chuckled.

'All the best' Suresh said. 'I am here for paper presentation.' It was written on his face.

'Paper presentation in a cultural program!' Chris was surprised.

'All the colleges in the state have merged the department symposiums with the cultural programs. That's because there are over 500 engineering colleges.'

'Oh! Time constrain.'

'Exactly'

'Again, all the best to you two'

'Same to you' we reached the college campus and waited for the people to get down before we could make a move. 'What is your paper about?'

'Ancient computer languages'

'That's outdated.' Chris said as Suresh frowned. 'As in, it sounds like a paper about forgotten history.'

'I won over 30 prizes for this paper.'

'Ok.' I smiled at a silent Chris. 'Sounds good. So today will be 31.'

'Yes.' Suresh said. 'The judge has assured me the first prize.'

I said nothing and paused for a moment. 'You mean to say you know the result before participating in the event. Are you the only participant?'

'You don't expect me to come all the way if I am not assured of winning.' He said and started walking quickly into the college campus.

'We travelled all the way even though we are not guaranteed a participant ID.'

'I am serious' He smiled. 'It just takes a phone call.'

'Fuck man.' I whispered to Chris. *Asshole has fixed the event and he is proud about it.*

'The fucker' Chris said. 'What about the guys who come expecting to give a good performance and win?'

'Their problem.' he replied. 'And by the way, the second spot is vacant.'

'Asses' I smiled. 'You know, we might be no different than rats.'

'Hmmm . . . . please explain.' He was confused.

'What do rats do?' I queried Chris.

'Come uninvited and take things away from the owner in the wildest way possible.' Chris answered. 'As of now, we have not taken anything from anyone.'

'But we might.'

'Psych' Suresh walked out of the scene.

'Have you ever seen these Hollywood zombie flicks?'
I asked Chris.

'A few, why?'

'Sometimes I feel nerds are zombies that don't kill.'

The college was huge and stood on 45 acres of land.
Banners were installed all around the campus, instructing
participants to move forward to the registration spot.
There were sign boards that kept the participants about
where and when the events were scheduled. The college
campus was very well constructed and compromised of
individual buildings with class rooms and laboratories for
each department, similar to St. Patrick.

'Well planned.' Chris stated.

'Yes.' I agreed. 'Rejo will be here any moment.' I
informed Chris. 'Our third team member.'

'Looks like you are the boss.' Chris was upset. 'Of all
the people in the world, it took a random idiot to be our
team member. I thought you were smarter.'

'You have not yet met him.' I reminded Chris. 'So
calling him an idiot sounds absurd. And after all, he is
all that I could get.' I paused for a moment and continued.
'Considering the fact that he woke me up at 4 am, comes
to show that he is interested. And you tell me one thing,
whom did you get?'

'Girls did not impress you.' Chris explained. 'And I
am new to the city and Jeffrey ensured that we did not
make very good friends in our class, except a few guys
who pee in context to participating and winning.'

'Listen, I understand what you are getting at, but it
is totally not my fault that we do not have friends who
support us in everything. You supported me, remember?'

'Right. So you got only Rejo?'

'Again, you have not even met him.'

'But he called you at 4 am. That scares me.'

'He will not open his mouth and will come and sit silently in a corner while we do the talking. I don't want a big mouthed bastard to control us.'

'Control you.'

'Alright.' I said. 'He was my school mate and a suppressed wannabe. He will work out well in our team.'

'You mean to say a dumb ass in the team for dumb-charades.' Chris finally agreed. 'Sounds okay to me.' He said. 'And with all due respect, what I understand is that we won't make it to the next round of any event that we participate in, no matter how many Titanic we get!'

'I would have to agree to that.' I smiled.

A fat boy came and stood next to me and Chris realized who that was.

'Rejo, good to see you.' I greeted him. Rejo smiled and said nothing.

'He remembers the deal.' I informed Chris. Rejo had a goatee and sleepy eyes. He would have easily weighed 100 kilos and had oval spectacles covering his eyes. 'He is a second year computer science student from TRR College of Engineering. He wanted to join St. Patrick College, but unfortunately he didn't make the cut.'

He looked around him with utmost fascination. 'Oh ok.' Chris replied.

Jeffrey came in the LSN college bus that functioned all around the city.

'If only I knew they allowed other college students to use their buses, we could have boarded their bus and come here.' I suggested Chris who frowned immediately 'Don't look at me like that. We would have not met those chicks if we would have not boarded the local MTC bus.'

'Right' Chris said 'Looks like Jeffrey and co. vanished in thin air'

'No . . . I saw them moving towards the registration desk as soon as they got into the campus.' I said.

Jeffrey and his gang saw Chris, Rejo and me but did not take any step of meeting us. But Jeffrey's expressions clearly showed that he did not like seeing me here.

'We have to bunk college while those assholes get OD.' I said sadly.

'I understand. If the college authorities had seriously understood talent, the list would have looked different.' Chris agreed.

'It is like looking at the tallest of all the kids out there and stating that *he will have the biggest dick of them all.* They don't know that Shorty has one of the biggest dicks in the porn industry.' I informed Rejo and Chris.

'Who is Shorty? Param eh?' Chris was curious.

'Are you seriously unaware of who Shorty is or are you acting dumb?'

'I am serious.' He replied.

'Fuck you' Rejo and Chris gave an expression as if he had never seen a porn movie in their life and their expressions were not convincing.

'By the way, your friend reminds me of Peter Griffin.' Chris said.

'Yeah!' I chuckled.

'Dude, there they come again!' Chris pointed to the two girls, who were still standing next to the registration desk. 'Looks like they are going to give their 100% in any event they participate in'

Rejo caught my shirt and smiled.

'The deal is still on. You can't talk.'

'They are my friends.' Rejo spoke.

'Deal over. Talk!' I said pulling Rejo's shirt towards me.

'Pink one is Shruthi and the green one is Preethi. Shruthi and Preethi are second year students in SRV College. Both are CSE students.'

'Computer chicks! Sisters?'

'No they are cousins.'

'Cool. So how do you know them?'

'I go for French classes and they are my class mates.'

'Ah . . .' I said. 'Bonjour!' I smiled.

'Bonjour.' He replied. 'Comment-allez vous?'

'I don't know further. So shut your mouth and get back to the topic. You talk with them?'

'Yes. They like me.'

'Do you think I'm mad to believe that?' I said quickly.

'Seriously dude. I am the topper in my French batch.' Rejo looked like he was stating the truth.

'Now I get it. You help them with the language don't you?'

'Yes. Help and that too only in studies! You guys might think in the wrong sense.'

'No . . . You are not like Chris and me to do that! By the way, why the fuck are you going for French classes? I know you find it tough to clear your semester papers. Then why French buddy?'

'My love for Languages'

'Kudos to you'

'Thank you' Rejo smiled 'By the way, who is Peter Griffin and why did you compare me with him.'

'He is a very sensible person who works for his family.'

'Oh. How do you know him?'

'Random'

'Ok'

'So' I put my hand over Rejo's shoulder. 'Why don't you go and talk with them now and introduce us to them?'

'I talk with them only during French classes.'

'Phone number?'

He said nothing and I got my answer.

'I think we can proceed to the registration desk. There are many like them here. We are wasting time expecting Rejo, your fucked up friend, to help us with any information.' Chris said.

I spoke no further and we moved towards the registration desk. My eyes were glued to Shruthi and Preethi, who were clearly looking for someone here. Surrounding them were many guys, who called themselves studs, who were staring at all the girls and raping them instantly with their eyes.

'*The registrations have started.*' The organizer was seated safely in an office and had a microphone to make the announcements. '*Please collect your forms and pay Rs.15 for every event you wish to attend.*'

There were over 1000 students flooding the 5 registration desks and Rejo volunteered to get into the crowd to buy the forms. Finally Shruthi noticed Rejo and she quickly came running towards him, pulling Preethi with her.

'Hi, Rejo' Shruthi came towards him. 'How are you?'

'I am good.' Rejo answered. 'How are you?'

'I am good too.' She turned to me and Chris. 'Your friends?'

'Yes. He is Justin, my school mate and this is his friend, Chris.'

'Hi.' Shruthi smiled at us.

Preethi said nothing and I was least bothered.

'Hi' I said happily.

'Nice to meet you two!' She turned back to Rejo. 'You bought the forms?'

Ah ha! I understood her intentions. She was searching for an ass who would buy her and Preethi the registration forms. Girls!

'Would you buy forms for the two of us also?'

'Of course he would' I pushed Rejo into the crowd. 'He is buying forms for us. He won't mind buying for you and your friend also. He loves buying forms for his friends. He will therefore not mind buying forms for you girls.'

'Stop blabbering' Chris whispered.

'So sweet of you' She turned to Rejo, not even handing over money to him, meaning he had to sponsor for the events they wanted to participate in.

'Get going fucker.' Rejo was pulled into the crowd. 'He is actually good.' I stated to Chris as I saw Rejo push his way to one of the registration desks within seconds. Shruthi and Preethi were busy whispering something. He came back with five forms and handed over two forms to the girls.

'Thanks a lot, Rejo. See you later.' Shruthi said.

'What are you girls going to participate in?' I asked them.

'Quiz is the only event that allows two to participate. The rest need three participants.' Chris caught hold of Rejo when Shruthi stated three.

'Ad-Zap needs five.' Chris smiled. 'Three and two makes five.'

Shruthi smiled. 'Provided we bomb in quiz' she left smiling.

'Provided . . .' I grinned 'They won't even qualify for the next round.'

'You might be wrong.' Chris said. 'And what about us?'

'Who created Computers?'

'Excuse me?'

'Ok, I told you quiz is out.' I smiled. 'Singing'

'Should we do it in a computer?'

'Ok, chuck that too.' We were pathetic. 'As planned previously Dumb-Charades is the event we will rock in.' I said.

'That's what you told in college. Sounds good' *Thank god!*

'Right' Rejo agreed.

'And ad-zap.' I added.

'We need 5.' Chris informed me. 'And I thought it was not on the cards.'

'Shruthi and Preethi will come bro, I am sure.' I was confident. Though physically I was there in that place at that moment, my heart was not with me, and my mind created scenes, quite similar to movie sequences. I was travelling in a car with Shruthi in the passenger seat and Preethi on my lap.

'Let me have Preethi.' Chris intervened. 'It is not fair for you to have both of them.'

'You too?'

'All guys think the same. The only difference being: you were driving in your mind while I was driving in my mind.' Chris grinned.

'Man. And I thought I was creative.'

'Ah! Poor you. The whole world is creative, but sadly they create the same scenes over and over again.'

'I would not mind participating in Ad-Zap with those chicks.' I informed Chris and Rejo.

'You mean the girls? I thought it is the same you who told me girls were someone you would never participate with?' Chris investigated.

'Is it recorded?'

'No.'

'So where's the proof?'

'Hmmm . . . So I was right.'

Chapter 7

The world's a stage?

August 2006:

Dumb charades was conducted in the AV—Hall of LSN College, Chennai.

Here it comprised of a person who mimed the words given to him and two other participants guessing it out in the given allotted time, making 3 participants mandatory for each team.

With time, dumb charades changed. People started using specific signs for each alphabet in the English language. And as time was a major deciding factor to differentiate the winner from the loser, everyone worked out tricks to find out the toughest word in matter of seconds, by using different and out of the world signs to point out different words. In other words, the person who mimed made the best use of his body and intellectual to help his team mates find any word, in matter of seconds.

'It should be easy for us. I know all the movies and actors.' I informed Rejo. 'You know the computer terms and Chris knows to act.'

'What about machines and famous sayings?' Rejo asked.

'Hmmm . . . let's stick to what we know.'

We were seated in the available seats at the back of the huge AV-hall.

'Hi' a gigantic person came running towards Chris and immediately pushed Rejo and me to the next few seats. 'Good day to you.'

'Hi author.' Chris smiled and gave his hand to the new guy, who had the LSN College ID card and an event organizer volunteer card too. 'This is Prithvin, the guy I told you.'

'Hi' I gave my hand and smiled 'I am Justin and this is Rejo. They are interested in buying your book.'

'This means I already have 2 clients early in the morning.' Prithvin said happily. 'Shall I give you the books now or after the event?'

'Hmmm . . . What is the price?' Rejo asked

'195rs.' Prithvin informed.

'195?' I asked him. 'I am really sorry but I have just 35rs with me now.'

'And I have just 20' Rejo added

'No issues. I accept cheque too.' Prithvin stated.

'Actually we are interested in buying your book, but not now. Maybe we will grab it from the nearby stores in the city.' I said politely.

'That's ok with me. Then all the best' He stated sadly and stood up.

'But you told me you are helping us win in dumb-charades?' Chris asked him.

'You know I don't help others in cheating. Play fair, win fair.' Prithvin left.

'That's a nice line. Guess you must know better guys to fix a competition. Like someone Suresh knows, who can help in winning in these events.' I said. 'But honestly, why are we talking about fixing now? If we give a really good performance on stage, no one can stop us from winning!'

'I need a member from each team, to come on stage and take a chit from the box.' Announced the girl dressed in salwar kameez, who undoubtedly, was the host for the dumb-charades event. Rejo went to the stage and took a chit out of a huge box. He came back to our place and showed it to us. It was numbered 45. 'Ok, please settle down in your respective places, so that we can run down the rules.' She announced. 'We will read it once and only once it will be.'

'Looks like we have enough time to practice the alpha codes!' Chris stated. 'As per the chit we are the 45th team to participate.'

After all the teams took their chits, the host stood up and read out the rules. 'I will call a number in random and the team with that number has to come and try out their luck here.' She concluded.

'So much for your philosophy!' Rejo kept his fingers crossed. 'Hopefully we are not the first to be on stage.'

She went to her desk and called out 'The first team on stage will be 45.'

'Oh oh' Rejo looked dead physically.

I said nothing and stood up, knowing that Chris and Rejo had their bums glued to the seat, both in a state of shock. 'We have come this far. We can't lose without participating.'

'We will lose even if we participate.' Chris cried. 'I always wanted to be first, but not here.'

'Believe me. We can do it.' I encouraged Chris. 'And no one will know even if we bomb.'

'I think you did not see Jeffrey, who is seated in the first row.' I turned and saw Jeffrey smiling at me. *That asshole is omnipresent*, I thought. *So is God!*

'Leave him alone, his team will be worse than ours.' I said confidently. 'He will give a shot at every event here and will win in none. Maybe someone must have misguided him into believing that if he participates in everything, he will win something!'

Chris looked at Rejo, who sank into his chair and was almost in tears.

'We did come to participate.' Rejo wiped his tears, got up from his place and stated. 'I am sure about one thing, first or last, we are here now and we must participate.'

'Awesome. That's the spirit.' I said as Chris got up with Rejo and we walked our way to the stage.

The host brought another box and said 'the enactor must take a chit and stand here while the other two participants get to sit in those chairs and guess the right answer. The total duration is 2 minutes. 30 seconds for the enactor to check the names and 90 seconds for their friends to guess.'

Chris and I sat in the chairs placed and Rejo took a chit out of the box. He looked into it and sported a dead look. 'Why is God unfair to us?' Chris whispered to me. I looked down at the audience and saw Jeffrey wishing us luck, with a smirk on his face. *As if he knew what was going to happen.*

30 seconds were up and Rejo started acting. 'What is that asshole doing?' Chris whispered. Rejo was holding his shirt and standing numb.

'Shirt?' Chris asked. Rejo immediately replied no and pulled his shirt again. We were staring at him for some time and could not understand anything. The host grinned.

Then, Rejo caught his long hair with his right hand and kept his left hand on his chest.

'This Chris is worse than any actor I have ever seen in my life. What the hell is he doing now?' And to our dismay, time was up!

Dejected, I got up from my place with Chris. The host came up to us and said 'That was pathetic!'

'I know.' I replied as Jeffrey chuckled.

We stepped down the stage and saw the next team take their position. I turned to Rejo and asked 'What were the words?'

'The first word was gentleman.'

'And what were you doing?'

'Showing that me in a shirt is the perfect example for a gentleman!'

'Fuck.' Chris stated. 'That is the dumbest thing I have ever heard.'

'And the second word?'

'John Abraham.'

'Fuck you.' I roared. 'I assume you caught your hair to show that you were similar to John Abraham?'

'I thought you would know.'

'Bloody fucker.' I turned towards Chris and apologized. He was ready to kill Rejo. 'I never expected this.'

'I understand Justin. I seriously do.' He kept staring at Rejo.

'So that's it. Are we going back home?' Rejo asked.

'Dance, music, drama: No chance.' I said sadly. 'Yes. But not a bye to cultural events' I replied with agony. 'You think we waited for over a year for this? I don't think so. We are worth more than this and I am sure this is just a start.'

'Inspiring'

'Believe me, better things are going to happen in the coming days, as my grandmother told me years back that all good things start on a bad note' I roared as we started walking out of the hall, as Jeffrey and his team mates, Jero and Jerome, laughed their ass out in the hall. 'Just wait and see, my friend, just wait and see.'

'You guys leaving?' Shruthi and Preethi were standing next to a food stall outside the AV hall.

'Yes.' Rejo smiled. 'We lost in Dumb-C and that was sadly the only event we came to participate in.' He stated. 'How about you girls?'

'We won in quiz.' Preethi finally spoke with interest. 'And we are taking home 2000 bucks!'

'You are wrong again.' Chris whispered.

'I know. Everything is going wrong around me.' I whispered back to Chris. 'Great!' I congratulated Shruthi and Preethi. 'So when's the treat?'

'We were thinking of giving a shot at Ad-Zap, since we have nothing else to participate in until the prices are distributed at 6pm, that is four hours from now.' Shruthi said. 'Sounds good?'

'Nice.' Chris said. 'So we are your team mates?' He asked, as I kept my fingers crossed.

'Yes, you guys!' Cheers! Something that sounded good to the ears.

'Alright' I smiled as I pushed Rejo and went close to Shruthi. 'Ad-Zap it will be.'

Rejo went across to the registration desk for Ad-Zap and brought back the form. 'We need a team name.' Rejo stated. 'College Champions?'

'We just now bombed in Dumb-C, you ass!'

'Oh ok.'

'Cult gurus?' Shruthi stated.

'Sounds fine' I smiled.

'I think that sounds similar as mine.' Rejo looked disappointed.

'All of us except you like it.' Chris, Preethi and Shruthi nodded. 'So it will be cult gurus.'

*   *   *

'Hi.' Shruthi wished the judge. She was engaging him in some conversation which he thoroughly seemed to enjoy.

Ad-Zap was an event which had a mix of marketing with gags. In this event, each team comprised of 5 to 8 participants (differed based on the college), and every team was given a certain imaginary comical product. The time given to each team was 5 to 10 minutes and the team had to market that product using jingles, scenes from movies and developing random ads to convince the audience and the judges we are the best marketers in the lot. Points were given to acting, speech delivery and comedy.

'So this is how they do it.' I whispered to Chris. 'I am sure she won in quiz the same way.'

'She actually did.' Chris replied back. 'Other teams got technical questions like equities, broking and similar shit whilst our beauties got w*hat is H2O? Who is Mahatma Gandhi?* I overheard a guy complain to some of his college friends.'

'That's bad.' I was surprised. 'No wonder the government wants to bring quota for women in every other job out there. The driving force for men in a job is clearly girls. They stay long to impress them and drop them home, pay thousands of rupees in gyms, go out to malls and posh restaurants even if their pockets are empty.' I started thinking. 'They even pay in thousands to watch a monkey fall in love with a blonde. How come all absurd creatures like monkeys and vampires end up falling in love with blondes?'

'Only God and the movie makers can answer that!' Chris replied.

'Ok, the judge told me that the product we have to advertise on stage will be Sarasu soap.' Shruthi said.

'Great.' I smiled. 'So what is our action plan?'

'I got a call.' Chris said, trying to get out of the scene.

'That's the tenth time you told me that today. Put the mobile in silent mode or better switch it off for the next 10 minutes, else your mobile will not survive the day.' I was pissed off by Chris. He was always engaged in his mobile and pulled out of the scene at times when the team needed him the most. This was the case in college also. I seriously doubted his actions. *A girl it must be!*

'You wouldn't say that if you were in my situation.' Chris said, as he hesitantly switched off his mobile.

'What's the plan?' I ignored Chris' concern.

'Simple. We will say that we look nice and the reason we look good is because of the soap.' Shruthi stated.

'Yeah!' Rejo stated. 'At last someone accepts the fact that we look great.'

'*We* refers to the girls, asshole!' I informed Rejo. 'Am I right?' I asked Shruthi.

'Yup' Shruthi smiled.

'And what do we have to do?'

'Stand and take pictures of our beautiful face and say *you girls look awesome!*'

'Let me give you a better idea.' I clearly did not like her idea. 'How about this? You girls were ugly in the beginning.'

'Ok' Shruthi frowned

'You use Sarasu Soap and end up becoming beautiful, got it?'

'Ok. We are the ok with the beautiful part, but not with the ugly part.'

'Rejo and Chris will be the ugly you!' I smiled but Rejo and Chris did not.

'Why don't you be the ugly chick?' Chris asked.

'I am the screenwriter. You guys are the artists.' I smiled. 'Some reason for you guys to be on stage.'

'I like this idea.' Shruthi stated, as Preethi also nodded her head in acceptance. Chris and Rejo had to succumb to it.

And so we took center stage. Rejo and Chris stood in front of the audience and asked them *Is there something we can use to become beautiful?*

I went running on stage and said *I have a solution. Here take this soap.*

Immediately they left the stage to show they were going to take a bath and out came Shruthi and Preethi. Their presence on stage was received with loud cheering. Shruthi then looked at me and exclaimed *Thank you for this soap. Sarasu soap works like magic!* She then raised the soap up, to be cheered by everyone seated there. The crowds, mostly comprising of single guys looking for a girlfriend, screeched "More, more, and more!"

Shruthi and Preethi cat walked around the stage and the whole crowd moved with them, as Chris, Rejo and I went backstage waiting for the girls to run down the clock.

'They are just walking around the stage and the crowd is cheering them.' Chris informed us. 'No wonder they pay millions to see actresses take bath on national television.'

Preethi suddenly slipped and fell on stage.

Oh my God! The crowd roared and all the guys rushed from their seats and tried jumping up to the stage to give her a helping hand, only to be promptly stopped by the bouncers. Preethi helped herself up to everyone's disappoint.

'How was it?' Shruthi asked me as the time was up, in no time!

'There is an advantage in being a girl, you must accept that!' We knew the results and it was confirmed 30 minutes after our performance. We won the first prize.

'We keep 1000 bucks each and you guys can share the 500 bucks.' Shruthi gave an evil smile.

'At least she did not take away our certificates.' Chris whispered.

'Ok.' I smiled. 'It was great working with you guys. When shall we meet next?'

'In some other cultural program for sure.' Shruthi said.

'There is one in Anand College, day after tomorrow.'

'Let's see.' Shruthi smiled and left with Preethi.

'Your numbers?' I asked boldly.

'Rejo has it.'

'Fucker' I turned to Rejo.

'I don't have it.' Rejo lied.

'You might be fat, but you are not scaring us. Give me those numbers or get yourself killed.'

Chapter 8

Ditch Chris

August 2006:

'**J**ustin, the principal wants to meet you.' The professor informed me. It was Computer networks session and the person handling the subject was Mrs. Matthew, one of the only few staffs who did not make Chris and me stand out during her sessions. The only person who stood out during her session was Deepakh. Actually he was the only person who stood out during all the sessions.

'What do you think it is for?' I whispered to Chris. 'Guess he wants to appreciate me for winning the first prize in the Ad-Zap event in LSN College!'

'Then he would have called me as well' Chris informed.

'True.' I got up from my place and went across to my professor.

'You have to go now.' She instructed.

'Ok.'

I walked out of the class and headed to the principal's room with the Principal's PA.

'Should I wait out?'

'He does not make culprits wait, thambi *(brother in Tamil)*.' He chuckled. 'You can go in.'

'Ok.' The term *culprit* did not go down well with me and I stared at him as I stepped into the room. 'May I come in Sir?'

'Immediately'

I walked slowly and stood next to him. He was close to fifty in age and weighed almost 140 I assumed. He was huge and had an aging moustache and no beard to compliment it.

'You are the ass who calls himself Justin, aren't you?'

'Yes. But why am I an ass, sir.' I asked innocently.

'Criminals like you are asses in my book.' He roared as the PA chuckled silently. 'It's a pity that I gave you a seat in this college, when so many worthy students had to go to colleges, less in stature than ours.'

I said nothing and did not understand why he was roaring at me. He had his laptop switched on and turned it towards me. 'What is this?' He asked me.

'A laptop sir'

He thought for a moment. 'I know that. Why do you use this for?'

Now I thought for a moment. 'For our personal use Sir' I said bluntly. 'In my case I use it to complete assignments, to watch movies, to listen to music and more' what *more* actually meant was porn and I was sure he knew that.

'And for internet?'

'Yes Sir, for internet also!'

'Open that Facebook site and show it to me.' He yelled.

I said nothing and typed the URL to access the Facebook login page.

'Facebook sir'

'Show me your webpage.' He roared.

I logged into my page and showed it to him.

'Not this, show me your webpage on Facebook.' He shouted.

'Which webpage sir?'

'The Facebook webpage that has all our college girls' pictures in it.'

I could not understand what he meant.

'Something with my college name as its heading.'

I finally understood what he was trying to say. I had created a group called "St. Patrick College 2005-09 batch" and added all the students who had an account in Facebook. I opened it and showed it to him.

'Ah. This is what they were telling me about.' He looked closely into the machine. 'From where did you get the girls' pictures?'

'I did not take it sir. They have their separate Facebook accounts and they like my page. So their main profile picture is displayed here.'

'I got to know that you hacked into all the student's computers and took their personal pictures and added it into your group.' *What a nut case!*

I stood silently.

'How dare you do something like when you are a student in my college?'

'Sir, but these girls themselves have added those pictures in their profiles. It's not my mistake that they like my page!'

'I don't want to listen to your stupid stories.' He shouted. 'Delete this group immediately.'

'You mean my page?'

'Whatever.' I deleted the God damn page and smiled. 'Sir, but the girls' pictures will still be online. Only the page is deleted from the Facebook database.'

'Ok then delete Facebook altogether.'

'I will have to get permission from Mark Zuckerberg to do that!'

'Tell him that I told you to delete it.' He roared. 'I don't give a damn about who he is. Get this Facebook deleted immediately.'

I clicked on the internet explorer close button and closed it, automatically closing Facebook and I smiled stating 'Sir I deleted Facebook.'

He turned the machine towards him and saw his desktop with no internet explorer. 'Good, now never do this again. And tell Mark Suckerberg that I will sue him if he tries to use my student's pictures again.'

'I will let him know that sir.' I smiled.

*   *   *

'So he praised you?' Jerome asked me.

'You know when I look at you and Jeffrey, I feel like I am looking at Thomson and Thompson.'

'Hmmm . . . . not funny!'

'Looks like you were expecting something else?' I asked them sternly. 'Maybe you knew what will happen, didn't you? You scripted it?'

'Not like that.' He blabbered. 'I just heard that someone had informed our principal about the Facebook page and all your friends. It was bad on your part to take up the initiative to create the group.'

'You guys did play a part in making me create a page on Facebook.' I was angry and Jerome was happy about that.

'You created the page, we joined. You are in no compulsion to listen to us, are you?'

'Yeah' I said no further, as Jerome left smiling. *Bastard!*

'That pig is bad bro. He knows nothing about anything.' Chris cooled me down.

'Are you referring to the principal or Jerome?'

'Both'

'I know. And the principal does not even know what it takes to delete Facebook. He thinks closing internet explorer will shut down Facebook forever.' I laughed out loud. 'He wanted me to threaten Mark Zuckerberg, can you beat that? Suckerberg'

'By the way he wants the college students to host a webpage for the college, which will include stuff only about him and his greatness.'

'You wrote about the college, but not about him, in your Facebook page.' Chris reminded. 'Guess that hurt him.'

'May be'

'So what plans for tomorrow?' Chris was interested in business. 'Are we going to Anand College?'

'You thought I was kidding when I asked Shruthi if she would come to Anand?' I asked Chris.

'Yes, since we already won an event in the big College, why should we go to a smaller one?' Chris stated.

'What other business do we have than to go and participate in cultural events?' I asked him.

'Join patcult committee?' He asked.

'With one winning certificate I don't think they will let us in. And now I am actually not very eager to join that committee. I would rather work parallel to that committee and participate wherever I want to, than to just go behind Jeffrey and a few fuckers and participate in places where they want us to.'

'You mean to say it is worth going?' Chris sounded interested.

'Of course. If you are interested, you are welcome to join me.' I smiled. 'And Deepakh too'

'He won't come for sure. It will take more than 5 winning certificates to convince a guy like that.' Chris exclaimed. 'Man, looks like you are totally into it. And honestly I am jobless.'

'So, tomorrow it will be.'

*   *   *

'That ass fucker Jones told my dad about my meeting with the Principal!'

'He likes doing that. Doesn't he?'

'But my parents laughed out loud, when they heard about it. Good to have parents who know Facebook.' I smiled. 'You think we should call Shruthi?' I asked Chris after having supper. I had my mobile in my hand. 'You think she will come?'

'Don't be a toothless tiger, be a ruthless tiger!' Chris said dramatically.

'Inspiring' I replied. 'So should I call her now?'

'Don't think twice.'

'I am finding it tough to dial the number.' I said.

TRING, TRING. The phone rang. 'Bloody hell!'

'Is it Chithra?' Chris shouted. 'Tell her that I just tried to commit suicide and am admitted in the hospital and will be out for 10 days'

'Chris!' I shouted. 'It is Shruthi.'

'Oh ok.' Chris was relieved. 'Thought for a moment it was Chitra. Because she gave me at least 10 calls over the past half an hour and I did not answer any.'

'Never heard about her from you?' I was surprised. 'Is she your girlfriend?'

'No. The person from whom I borrowed 250 bucks when we left for LSN College two days ago' He smiled.

'I did not remember you meeting anybody?'

'You watched memento yesterday right. Short term memory loss happens to all.'

'Hmmm . . .'

'She was my school mate and the only person in this world who lends me money.' He kept his fingers crossed and I knew he was lying. Finally I understood who kept calling him all day long. *My God, even Chris has a girlfriend!*

89

'How does she have my number?'

'I gave it to her. She said she wanted my friends' numbers so that she can call them in case of any emergency.'

'Ok.' I said. 'Now what do I do about this call?'

'Simple.' Chris smiled. 'Answer'

I looked at the answer key for over five seconds in my mobile and finally pressed it. 'Hello.'

'Shruthi. Tomorrow 9 am, Anand College. Don't bring Chris along and not Rejo for sure.' And she cut the phone immediately.

'That's it?' Chris roared out. 'Man, that's not cool. But what did she say?'

'Don't bring Chris along and not Rejo for sure'.

'Fuck' Chris roared.

'I think she believes I am the MAN!'

'That's not funny. Why the hell does she want you to ditch me?'

'There must be something into this plan.' I thought. 'She is planning big.'

'Anyways I am coming. I don't need any bitch to instruct me what I should do.'

'Yes.' I was disappointed. 'She is faster than a rocket. She did not even give me time to talk.' I paused for a moment. 'Anyways, we are going tomorrow and with those girls in my team, we are winning for sure.'

*   *   *

'Dude, I am so happy you willingly agreed to give me the opportunity to participate in Dumb-Charades with Shruthi and Preethi.'

'I was not given an option.' Chris did not smile.

'Now I understand why they did not want you to accompany me all the way to this college. They don't have ad-zap here. You might as well sit and watch us participate. I cannot assure you that we will win, but we will surely give our best shot.'

'I'd rather go back home.' Chris said. 'Unless you agree to pay for my lunch, which you will do, whether you win this event or not!'

'Done'

I walked up to the stage with Shruthi and Preethi.

'Let Preethi be the enactor.' I told Shruthi. 'She hardly talks.'

Preethi said nothing and went to take a chit from a box. The rules were similar to the ones framed in LSN College.

'Hope we get three easy words to guess.' I whispered to Shruthi. 'By the way, why did you opt for me over Rejo and Chris? We conversed with each other for just a few minutes! Guess you have fallen for me.'

'I wanted you to be in my team because you looked like the dumbest from the three.' Shruthi said boldly. 'Don't dream. You are not eligible to even be my brother.'

'That's not polite.' I added nothing. 'Let's not share what we spoke now with anyone else.' Jeffrey and his gang bagged OD for this competition and were present in the hall. In LSN College, Jeffrey's team was as bad as mine. They were given words like "Noah's ark" for which Jerome kept shaking his head (to depict "no" I guess) and "fast and furious" for which Jerome kept running all around the hall.

'Hi.' Preethi spoke to the host (a guy). Since the cultural events were open to students of all colleges, the hall was over flowing with participants. 'Please give me easy words.' She put her pen down in front of the host and leaned down to pick it up. *His heart skipped a beat*, I thought.

'Ok.' He sweated and immediately wrote some words in a chit and gave it to her.

'30 seconds for the enactor to check the words and 90 seconds for the enactor to act it out.' He said. 'Is 30 seconds enough, dear?' He asked Preethi slowly.

'He he' Preethi smiled.

'She is skilled.' I whispered to Shruthi. 'But not as talented as you!'

'Thank you.' She smiled, happy with the compliment.

The event began and Preethi pointed to her eye.

'Eye?' Shruthi asked and Preethi nodded. That was surprisingly our first word!

Whoa! I don't believe this is happening

Then Preethi pointed to her watch.

'Watch' Shruthi roared and that was the second word.

Finally Preethi pulled her hair.

'Hair' Shruthi said.

'Excellent.' The crowd booed the host. But the host was not bothered as he gave his hand to Preeethi and applauded her. 'You guys found out all the words in 8 seconds. A new record and you guys have already won the first prize, as I am sure that there is no one in this hall who can better that.'

There are advantages in being a girl and I am seeing it. I thought. *No wonder there are people queuing up in Mumbai clinics to undergo that sex change operation.*

'That was bad.' Jeffrey came out from the crowd and shouted. 'We got *Caligula, pretentious disorder* and *whisper in the dark is as good as the sunlight in the morning.* And this team gets *eyes, watch* and *hair?'*

'Happy to see you here Jeffrey' I shook hands with Jeffrey 'though you don't seem to be in a good mood, it is great to have you here.'

'I'm not talking to you' Jeffrey ignored me.

'I should be saying that. Because this is the second time in as many days that you assholes got OD and we did not win. But I won't complain because I will be back in college with the winning certificate.' I shouted.

'It's based on the chit you get.' The host defended himself. 'You can't question us.'

'This is how the show works.' I informed Jeffrey.

'Guess I will install artificial boobs the next time I come to participate here.' Jeffrey blabbered in anger.

'That won't suit you.' I laughed out loud.

'Try me' Jeffrey exclaimed.

'Don't tell me you are going next week to Mumbai for that!' I answered back.

'Fuck you' Jeffrey said and moved out 'And to these pathetic organizers. I am sure this is what will happen to you guys when you travel to other colleges for participating.'

'Is he cursing them?' I asked Chris.

'Yes' Chris chuckled.

'We make a good team.' I informed Shruthi, as Jeffrey left with Jerome and Jones, his losing partners.

'Excuse me?' Shruthi asked.

'As in, you guys make a good team.' I surrendered.

'That's better.'

I smiled. 'But we do have a role to play in your success.'

'You completed our team. That's it.' Shruthi had pride written all over her face.

'But you called me to be your team mate and not Chris or Rejo' I shouted in front of Chris.

'Ha! Don't live in your luck. It won't even last a week.' She grinned.

'I don't understand?' I seriously did not understand.

'You will.'

'What's your share for today?' Chris asked me.

'200 bucks.'

'Out of 1000 bucks?'

'They like the number four.'

'You referring to something else, are you not?'

'No no.'

'Alright'

'We are not interested in participating in quiz this time around. Have to leave early for a family function. Bye.' Shruthi and Preethi ran out of the college.

'So what about me? I go empty handed?' Chris looked devastated.

'At least you lost nothing out there. But we can still participate in the western dance competition. We have already won here once. We can call the three J's to be our team mates.'

'I would have said a yes for Rejo, but not for them.' Chris answered. 'You did not call him, did you?'

'He is preparing for his semesters.'

'But that's five months from now. His semesters fall on the same dates as ours, right?'

'On the same day' I informed him. 'He needs five months to study what a normal human can in a month.'

'That's called talent I guess. But on a serious note, people do struggle with studies. It is an inborn curse.' I said. 'There are only 6 IIMs in India and over a million students aspiring to join there. So it is not possible for all to make the cut.'

'And parents should realize that.'

'Correct. And not all kids who could not make it to the IIMs NOT write a book.'

'The voice of 1000s of authors who wrote a book and have not sold a copy!'

'Big time' I chuckled. 'Anyways, the three J's or home?'

'Empty handed sounds bad and so I'll choose the three Jackasses. Your call?'

'Jackasses it will be.' I roared. 'But will they accept.'

'They might. I understand Jeffrey hates me, but with him in the losing side, I don't think he might not be interested in winning something here, even if he has to join hands with me. Simply because he might be interested in PAYBACK!'

Chapter 9

The challenge

September 2006:

'**Y**ou dog!' I roared at Jerome. 'You can't even stand in front of a crowd for a moment without wetting your pant?'

Jerome looked around and started crying.

'I think you pressed the buzzer.' Chris whispered. 'I better move out of this scene. My mother did not send me to college to get hit by different pairs of torn shoes.' Jeffrey came forward with his _terror gang_.

'How many did you win?' Jeffrey roared.

'Two and counting.' I replied.

'That's just two then.'

'But I am going to add more to it.'

'And how many have you won without the help of your GIRL friends?' He shouted as hard as he could.

'It's nature's gift for God's sake.' Chris corrected Jeffrey.

'Out of context. I am talking to your friend who ditched you for winning in dumb-charades.'

'He has a point.' Chris smiled and stood behind Jeffrey, behind whom the whole class stood.

'Nothing for now' I answered.

'Nothing in the near future too, I'm sure. They use their GIRL THING to get the awards and you just participate to complete the team.'

I said nothing. He was right.

'And how dare you insult my friend and blame him for losing in the dance event.' Jeffrey said. 'You asked him to stand in front of a mad crowd and do crazy stuff which no one will do.'

'Crazy stuff?' I laughed out loud. 'All that I asked him to do was to stand and say *Hello Everybody* but he went on stage and pissed!'

'Yes,' Jeffrey babbled. 'You can masturbate when you want to, but you cannot answer nature's call when you want to. It comes when it wants to.'

'Using lot of wants will not make the guys want to help you.' I chuckled.

'You guys accept it?' Chris asked the class tentatively.

They thought for a moment.

'Obviously no one will piss on stage unless they are not taught how and where to piss.' I shouted.

'There were 3000 people in the hall.' Jeffrey informed them.

The whole class started murmuring.

'I willing pee if I am fronting of that big a crowd.' Arun S said. 'It is mistaking in your part to making Jerome stand there.'

'Even Jeffrey will pee. No wonder you made me send Jerome.' I added.

'Win without any help from Shruthi or Preethi.' Jeffrey chuckled.

'That's a challenge?'

'I suppose yes. If want to show the world that you have a little brother down there.'

'I will show my little brother only to my wife, not to the world.'

'Oh yeah! Do it.' He roared.

I stared hard at Jeffrey. 'That's a sick challenge.'

'Ha ha!' Jeffrey laughed along with the crowd. 'The person who takes shelter under a girl's dupatta is talking.'

They left, except for Chris, Deepakh and Param and some others who wanted to know more.

'So you guys did not dance?' Param asked. Param, as stated before was a movie buff and he found a trust worthy friend in Prasad, another shorty without moustache, in my class. Both of them loved movies and thanks to torrents, they had access to all the movies in the world.

'They played a movie song and we were asked to go on stage. And a representative from our team was requested to go on stage before the team performed to introduce the team and inform the crowd what dance we were about to perform.' I replied.

'Oh' Prasad said 'and I assume Jerome was that person?'

'On target! He volunteered for it. He did not return backstage for over five minutes, after which the host informed us we were disqualified and that we were banned from participating in any event in Anand College, all thanks to Jerome wetting the stage' I exclaimed. 'Thankfully I got my dumb-charades certificate and prize money before the event started.

'Ah!' Param said 'And Jeffrey complains that you are at fault.'

'Hmmm . . .'

'I understand. Look at it in a positive sense. If you guys danced on stage, they would have banned our college for lifetime.'

'Valid' I smiled 'that's why I kept quiet when Jerome volunteered to go on stage to introduce his team. We did not even hire costumes nor did we have an audio track! We requested the DJ to play any song he liked and we would dance accordingly'

'Whoa!' Chris smiled 'Master plan!'

'Did you even think you will ever win this such a MASTER PLAN?' Deepak asked

'We tried and are still alive'

'Yeah'

'But now, my master plan has backfired.' I cried. 'Those fuckers in patcult committee have already informed the department staff that I am taking the help of other college students to win in events and so they have issued a notice to all, specifically stated that if they find me or any other student participating with students from other colleges in the near future, I will be banned from participating in cultural events again in my life.'

Chris looked shocked. 'How did you get into this?'

* * *

'You know this challenge sounds more like that movie with that actress, who could break open any safe with ease.'

'What is the use of a safe when you cannot use the money inside it?'

'You can buy speakers that can blow away any girl's clothes!' Chris exclaimed. 'It happens only in movies like the Italian job. But I thoroughly enjoyed it. If only they would have focused on the girl than the hero, the audience would have appreciated that scene totally.'

'And you know what, I messaged Shruthi stating that I will not be able to join her in any more competitions again.'

'And what did she reply?'

'Who's bothered?' I cried.

'I am bothered, man. What did she reply?'

'That was her reply. *Who's bothered?*'

'Oh. Sad' Chris felt for me. 'And I assume you would have messaged her back texting, *can we be just friends?* right?'

'Perfect man'

'And she would have texted back, *fuck you.*'

'No'

'Then what did Shruthi text back?'

'*Suck you*' I paused for a moment and started again. 'How did I get into this Chris?' I cried out loud.

'You tell me. You sound like a guy who is charged for murder.' Chris replied. 'This is the dumbest challenge put forward by anyone around. *Win without those girls!* They sounded like it is the toughest in the world.'

'I know.' I said. 'But it is a challenge none the less.'

'This is something you must not break your head on, I tell you.' Chris was casual. 'We, or if the challenge means just *you*, can go to any pathetic unknown college where hardly anyone comes to participate and win as many prizes as possible and tell them *I did it.* You needed Shruthi and Preethi because it was LSN and Anand.'

'Hmmm . . . that's true.' I thought about it. Chris had a point. There were over 500 colleges in Tamil Nadu. Not many students would bother going to each and every college to participate in cultural. As all the colleges did conduct competitions, I could actually win somewhere and eventually win in the challenge put before me. And by the way, before Shruthi and Preethi, it was only Chris and me! And obviously girls can wait. I honestly spoke a lot about chicks and the interest I had in them, but the fact was I was never into it. I, like many, was bothered about cultural. *Girls will come with time,* I was confident.

'But how do we find the competitions that are coming up in those colleges?' I asked Chris.

'You should be bothered about it, not me.'

*   *   *

'Are you staying here for dinner again?' My mother, as usual, was irritated by Chris' presence in my house during dinner time.

'It's 8 already aunty.' Chris gave an innocent look. 'My parents have told me not to step out of any of my friend's house empty stomach, after 7:30pm.'

'That's the most pathetic lie I have ever heard in my life.' My mother said. 'You made that up?'

'No no.' Chris assured. 'And I don't doubt the credibility of my parents' statements. I do everything that my parents want me to do.'

'I think they asked you to study well and score a minimum of 85% in any exam you take up and you have not shown any interest in doing that. So you have restricted yourself in doing some.'

'I would not put it that way. 85% is ridiculous.' Chris giggled. 'You would never tell Justin to do that.'

'Why are you pulling me into this, Chris?' I answered quickly.

'For a cup of rice and fish curry' Chris giggled again.

My mom walked out of the room, slamming the door on her way out.

'You know I actually completed reading the Old Testament from The Bible.'

'That's awesome. Now you are talking like a Catholic.'

'Yes. I noticed that in majority of the books in the Bible people attacked and destroyed other nations for two things' I said.

'Cattle and water?'

'No, for money and women'

'That's normal. Now, politicians and priests do the same.'

'There would have been thousands of you and me at that time I guess.' I said.

'You mean to say you will kill for money and women. Man that is dumb, I thought we were better than that.'

'You would have killed for the goat, I for the women.' I giggled.

'I would have died if not for your parent's food.' Chris murmured. 'My grandmother cooks food that even rats do not care to consume. If only Hitler knew about her, he would have appointed her as the head chef for his concentration camps.'

'But your grandfather did survive the past 50 years consuming it. So honestly, I call it exaggeration.'

'Ah . . . he cooks for himself, if you are not aware. And she also consumes the food my grandfather cooks.'

'Then why does she cook for you?'

'God knows.'

'I have told you to be good to them.'

'I remember.' Chris paused. 'So what are your plans for the coming days? Any luck with culturals?'

'I spoke to Rejo after college today evening. He told me about some college called IRON that is going to conduct their annual cultural program next week.'

'IRON? That's an absurd name for a college. Who the fuck would even imagine a name like that for a college?'

'An asshole?'

'Valid.' Chris laughed. 'So are you going for it?'

'Of course, yes! I can shut Jeffrey's big mouth by winning a prize from that place.' I said. 'I'll get to win the challenge in a week.'

'True.' Chris thought for a moment. 'But what if you lose out there?'

'That's dumb. IRON is too dumb a name for a college. I don't think anyone will even be there other than you, me, mosquitoes and other pests.'

'I will slap you if you are wrong.'

'Slap me twice if I am wrong.'

*   *   *

'Slap me twice, Chris.'

Chris slapped me so hard that I knew I was not dreaming.

'Take your word back.'

'I will.' I was stunned, seeing what stood in front of me.

'It was for obvious reasons that you underestimated this college to have a bad program, but I doubted the fact that people think alike.'

'Believe me. I never ever thought I will see this.'

Though the college comprised of only one rusty building, it had no shortage of participants.

'Shall I put a number?'

'You will put 2000, if I am not wrong.'

'I was thinking of 3000.'

'That might be valid. There is hardly any space for even a mosquito to get to the registration desk.'

'You think all of them were challenged by a little known Jeffrey?' Chris sounded suspicious. 'My mother told me when I was young that: there are seven people in this world, who look alike, talk alike and behave alike. Now I believe her. There seems to be a Jeffrey in every engineering college.'

'Looks possible' I guessed. 'But it was you who told me that I can easily win in this college, because it is unknown. Looks like unknown is known to everybody! There were hardly 1000 in LSN College.'

'Dude, we are still close to the out gate. Your call'

'Why do you always put me in the hot seat? You take the call.'

'I would say the bus back home will be reaching the bus stop in some 10 minutes. I will sponsor for the tickets.' Chris smiled and started walking.

Chapter 10

The Book Fair

<u>*October 2007:*</u>

'One whole year and 8 different colleges.' I sighed. 'Two full semesters have gone by and I have won nothing. Some sort of a challenge I took up. And it also cost all my holidays.' I cried. 'It all started with IRON College. So dumb of me to participate in a college like that. Thanks to you, fucker.'

'Don't blame me.' Chris defended himself. 'It is not my mistake that you ended up participating there. Who told you to go and talk in English on stage there for role play?'

'You knew that the college cultural theme was *strictly Tamil*, right?'

'I did not know about that.'

'And bloody I got disqualified there, simply because I stepped into Shakespeare's shoes and spoke in English, not knowing that any character we took up must talk in Tamil.' I was devastated. 'You know what: I never knew that Shakespeare could speak in Tamil.'

'His plays are made into movies in regional languages right?' he stated.

'Right' I agreed. 'Two years we spoke a lot about cultural, chicks, babes, darlings, hotties . . .'

'In short girls'

'Yes girls. And about rocking in cultural events, making a name for ourselves' I thought hard. 'Look now where we are and where our experiences have brought us to.'

'To a book fair!' Chris murmured. 'You think reading books will help you win?' Chris and I were surfing through the ocean of books kept in the one of the stalls. It was the annual book fair in Chennai and over 1000 book vendors had set up stalls. They sold books ranging from fiction, comics, non-fiction, to autobiography, cooking, travel and college text books.

'Of course yes. Books are inspiring. Remember the last book I recommended to you.'

'You recommended Wrinkle digest to me.' Chris frowned. 'Saying it comprised of moral stories.'

'And it had moral stories, right?'

'My foot! I read the same stories printed in the 2005 edition in the 1995 edition of wrinkle. They have just added more color and graphics to the new edition.' I said. 'And they changed the village too'

'Who told you to wrinkle regularly?'

'My mistake'

'If you had not read all the books, wrinkle digest would have succeeded in cheating you with the new edition, as they have been doing with their new readers.'

'Hmmm . . .'

'Ok' I grinned. 'So the book I need is the one that will inspire and motivate me to win in any challenge put in front of me.'

'Yes. But those books will easily cost you at least a hundred.'

'Chris, I brought 100 bucks with me.' I smiled. 'I am prepared.'

'Great. You browsed online for the best seller among motivational books?'

'Actually no'

'Anyone recommended you any book?'

'I am a self-made man.' I hid my ignorance.

'Fuck man. So you are going to randomly pick up some book and leave?' Chris asked.

'Yes'

'Alright, your money, do what you want with it' He smiled. 'You know I updated my status on Facebook.'

'To what?'

"Sachin is the human form of the living God in this cricket frenzy country. So why do we have to wait for the second coming of Christ?"

'That's a mad status you put up. Anyone liked it?'

'156'

'How many friends do you have?'

'157'

'Even the Christian guys like Chacko and Jose liked that?'

'For your kind information, they don't have an account in Facebook.'

'They have accounts in Facebook!'

'But they are not in my friend list.'

'Their friend lists includes their gang members and over 100 friends with the name Jesus Christ.'

'You mean to say anyone with the name Jesus Christ is on their list.'

'Yes. And surprisingly guys with that name have given their location as Afghanistan.'

'Oh'

'Must be some random terrorists with fake accounts'

'Why would they do that?'

'To play mafia wars' I chuckled.

'Except me all of them liked it? Crazy' I continued 'and my status was "Make a note of these helpline numbers. You might need them at times of need."'

'And how many liked it?'

'Ten of them are missing from my friend's list. And two pinged me *"Fuck my number"*'

We stepped into one of the book stalls and browsed through the books.

'You have any recommendations?'

'Someone told me about a book that inspired him, but I forgot the name of the book.'

'Thank you. You could have rather said NO.'

'Look at this book.' Chris picked up a book and showed it to me. *How to say No, when you have to say no.*

'No, thanks.' Chris kept the book back in the rack.

'How about this one? *100 easy ways to win a match.* That's what we are looking for, right?'

'It says MATCH.' I looked at a book and picked it up. 'This costs just 10 bucks.'

'But it says *"The best Sexual positions."* I thought you wanted to buy some motivational book.' Chris stared. 'And it looks used too. Someone has already tried this book and returned it back.'

'He or she must have memorized the positions.' I smiled. '10 bucks won't hurt my pocket.'

'You better open the book and check a few pages.' Chris looked embarrassed. 'In public, I will not check such books.'

'I can see that little kid checking *"Kama sutra"*.'

'You can't convince me.'

'But it will hurt your reputation.' An old lady crossed us and stared with disgust at me.

'Believe me, I don't know him.'

'Spoilt brats' she murmured and left.

'Forget her. Let's take it. It will help us in the future.' I said.

'You have forgotten the reason why we are here. *Motivational Book!*'

'Take some random book for 90 bucks or less. I am not letting go of this book. This is a bargain.' I kept it in my basket.

'Ok.' Chris replied. I kept staring at the book in my basket. 'How about this? *"Win and win like a man"* by Wilkin'

'Sounds masculine' I smiled.

'And it's just 50 bucks.' Chris informed. 'And it says you will get a chance to meet the author if you buy the first copy of this book.' He said as he checked the back cover 'It says this book is the first book!'

'Great. So the book was launched today.'

'If today was twenty years ago! Great, we get to buy the first copy after twenty years from the day the book was launched. Awesome, some book we are buying.'

'Take it man. People don't know the value of good books.'

'Not as much as you know.' Chris grinned. 'You go pay for your books while I check the rest of the books. I might as well pick one for me.'

'What genre are you looking for?'

'Something that will help me find better friends.'

*   *   *

Be sure you want to open this book. Oh God, yes! 'I bought you so that I can read.' I laughed when I opened the A-Rated book that I bought a few hours ago.

It would have been better if it had pictures with description of the positions shown I thought. 'Now I need to use of lot of my imagination.' I flipped to the first page only to find a small sheet with some writing on it.

'Wow! Someone's actually written his experiences after reading this book.'

I grew anxious and read the paper. *Only an ass will buy this book.*

'Ok.' I kept the sheet down and started reading the book.

This book is certified by the writers association of India as a book that can be read by readers of all ages. To ensure that everyone can read this book; the association has made lot of changes to the book.

FOR ALL AGES? I grew suspicious and flipped to the first chapter.

"Aaja, aaja" My mobile rang. I picked it up and saw the screen display Rejo's name.

'Why the fuck is he calling me now?' I thought for a moment.

I switched off my mobile and got back to my book.

Chapter 1: Things to be remembered before having sex.
Praise be to Lord for making me a human being and giving me an opportunity to live in this wonderful world. It is with great honor I present to you my book, sexual positions.

....

....

....

....

....

These are the things to be remembered before having sex.
Now, moving to the second chapter.
Position No. 1 *********

....

....

....

....

....

This is the favored and the most preferred position among first timers.

'FUCK' I threw the book. Hundred censored pages? There was nothing written in the book.

'No wonder it cost me just 10 bucks. It makes me do the writing and explore the positions myself.' I sighed in frustration.

"Why don't you try me?" WIN AND WIN LIKE A MAN called out to me.

This book won't bite me for sure. I thought and took the book in my hand.

Written by Wilkin, the most promising author of the modern world.

'Yeah right! I get to buy his first book after 20 years. Very promising, indeed.'

I would like to thank the people who inspired me to write this book.

'Must be his girlfriend for sure.'

My parents and Steve

'Whoa! Not a girl. Gay'

This book will help you plan for your future.

'I am not reading the prologue.' I told myself.
The book had 11chapters.

CONTENTS

1. *Never take a competition for granted. There are wolves everywhere who know how to win.*
2. *Never go for small things. You will not get it. Aim big.*
3. *Take the dogs out for a walk. They will pee in the street and wag their tail in joy.*
4. *Stand alone and win alone. A team is scary!*
5. *Look at doing things which others will not do.*
6. *Spend cash and spend smart.*
7. *Plan for a year and not for a day.*
8. *Keep your mouth shut when it matters the most.*
9. *Take the right moves at the right time.*
10. *Know that you are THE MAN!*
11. *Thank you for buying the book.*

'Hmmm . . . . This book runs for just 65 pages. So let's see what the author has to say.' I moved to the first chapter.

I sat down in my chair placed in front of my table and started reading the first chapter closely.

*   *   *

'So you studied all the sexual positions?' Chris asked me sarcastically. 'Actually if you have, whom are you going to try it out on?' He laughed out.

'I did learn a lot.' I smiled. 'And I learnt one thing which I am going implement right away.'

'With whom?' Chris asked suspiciously.

'Don't be scared.'

'Eh?'

'I read the other book. Sexual positions book was shit. Wasted 10 bucks. The other book was good.'

'Oh . . . so it has motivated you to do wonders?' He grinned.

'No. It has motivated me never to buy a motivating book again.'

'Ah! I told you go for a good one.'

'And you know what. I finished the book in one sitting and in an hour.'

'What did it say?'

'Everything necessary to demotivate me. One of the chapters was titled Aim Big and it said if you flunk in a paper in a semester, make sure you don't flunk in not more than one the next semester. That is Aim big it seems! Man now I am as down as ever!'

'You must have realized that the minute you took that book. No wonder no one touched it for the past 20 years.'

'I know' I felt dejected. 'Deepakh will know better' I turned to Deepakh who was busy digging into his book at the class entrance. It was no surprise that Alvin took a subject every semester, as he was regarded as one of the best staffs in the department and all the students in the department voted for him. Even Chris, Deepakh and I voted for him regularly, as he was the only staff who made sure that he corrected papers in such a way that no one flunked. For a department flooded with staffs who corrected papers in a way that everyone flunked, he was an exceptin. 'You go to book fairs regularly right?'

'Right' Deepakh smiled

'Do you seriously think reading books help us?'

'It helps people who want to be helped.' He said. 'It is not like marriage, where you can compromise and go for a girl available in the market and tinker them. Books must be selected carefully as content is most important in each and every book bought. Book with little detail is as good as a book with nothing. In simple terms, I cannot buy a

C language book and learn Java from that. I must buy a book that has Java in it.'

'So what do you think will inspire me to get back on track to winning ways in cultural competitions?'

'Honestly we never won in cultural competitions!' Chris corrected me.

'Maximize your strong areas and minimize your weakness.' Deepakh stated.

'And how do I do that?'

'Simple.' Deepakh kept his hand on my shoulder and said 'I donno.'

'That helped'

Chapter 11

The Letter

<u>*November 2007:*</u>

'It's been two and a half years now since you first met me and you have not yet told me, neither about who Chitra is nor about what she is to you.' I asked Chris. The best part in my college was that the block in-charge identified a few individuals and labeled them as culprits, and did not bother about the rest of the guys in the class. In my class, Param and Fahd Ahmed were labeled as culprits and their duty was to report in the detention classes whenever required. The block in-charges had to show a number to the college Director that these many guys were caught on that day and Param and Fahd volunteered from my class.

'Fahd raised a request to meet a girl right?'

'Yes' I smiled. 'He wanted to propose to Shazia and wanted the college to grant him permission.' I paused and continued. 'Chitra?'

'She is my friend'

'Girlfriend'

'A girl who is your friend is your girlfriend.' Chuckled Deepakh 'I would also love to meet her.'

'Let her be just your friend.' I said 'Won't you introduce her to your friends. We won't eat her for sure and you know that. We love to socialize!'

'Hmmm . . .'

'What is she doing here?'

'Studying'

'Please arrange a good dinner for our gang.' Deepakh pleaded. 'The cult gurus'

'So much for the name.' I said sadly. 'Nothing seems to happen right for us.' I paused 'And above all we have you' I pointed to Deepakh 'who has never accompanied us to any cultural festival.'

'That's because I am always busy'

'Busy my foot, fucker' I roared as Deepakh said nothing. Unlike other sessions, all of us were seated inside the class (to Deepakh's disappointment) in Prof. Charan's class (who took System software), who did not believe in making students stand out during his session, no matter what crime they commit.

'Please be low.' He requested us. 'I am not able to take the session.'

'Sorry sir.' I apologized. He was right. The class buzzed like a fish market, all discussing about the upcoming Industrial Visit to some company.

I leaned forward. 'Hi, Fahd'

'Class is going on.' Fahd replied without turning back.

'Ok. I know that.' I smiled. 'I wanted to ask something important about the industrial visit that the department is planning to organize in the coming month of January.'

'What about that?' He turned back and asked. He was as skinny as me and was also a mallu from Calicut. He was a bit shorter than me and had a lot of facial hair.

'What's the spot?' I asked him eagerly.

'Success technologies'

'You must be joking.'

'What do you mean by JOKING?'

'That's like just about a kilometer from our campus. We can go walking.'

'It's an IT company for God's sake. IV is conducted once a year so that the students can get a picture of what's in store once they take up a job in any of these companies.'

'Ok. What if the company is Futura technologies?'

Param lent his ear to our conversation and immediately turned back. 'That's funny. Futura is in Bangalore and they will never send us there. And above all, Futura technologies will not invite us for an industrial visit to their campus. We know no one there.'

'What if they send us there?'

Chris looked surprised. 'You sound like you can do it.'

Arun S turned and joined the group. 'Whoa! Are you serious?'

And so the news spread.

"Success technologies" has been the major recruiter in my college because it is owned by the same person who runs our college. So when I spoke of something other than that, especially something which included a trip to a completely new city, it sounded fresh for the students in my class.

'Dude' Param started. 'It will be kickass if you can actually pull it off.'

'It is one time of our college life, when we can actually talk with chicks without raising a request.' Fahd added

'I know' I agreed.

Param was excited. 'I thought you were joking when you spoke about that over the phone yesterday.'

'Now you know I was not.'

'Yes. It will be one hell of a trip up north to Bangalore.'

'I know, Param.' I smiled.

'How are you going to make this happen?' Prasad asked me.

'I was thinking about the same.'

'I understand' Chris said 'I think there are a few who are already ready to help you.'

'And I thought all of these guys stood against me.'

'They never stood against you. And even if everyone stood against you, when things matter, Indians get together.' Chris reminded

'No wonder we have states with different languages.' Deepakh added.

'But still use English as the medium of instruction in all the schools and colleges.' I said.

'Though it is the language spoken by the people who controlled and tortured us for so many years, it helps us communicate with people from different states.' Chris said.

'It mainly has to do with our future.' I informed.

'You mean DEPENDENCY?' Deepakh asked.

'In MNCs'

'But MNCs include Indian companies too.'

'How many Indian companies use Hindi as their medium of communication?'

'English men don't speak Hindi, for your kind information.'

'But they watch Bollywood flicks.'

'And how many Bollywood movies are original?'

'Hmmm . . .'

'What hmmm?'

'Hmmm . . .'

'Fuck you.'

'I used hmmm cause I don't know the answer. So please let me know.'

'They check on the Bollywood movies to check which director has copied their movie. It may be just a scene or the entire film.'

*   *   *

From,
The director,
St. Patrick College of Engineering,
Chennai.
To,
The manager,
Futura technologies,
Bangalore.

Sir,

Our students are sent to various companies in and around India to understand and get an idea about how a company works and what kind of opportunities are there in store for them, once they get into the industry.

This year we have decided to send them to Bangalore and have provisionally selected your company as the only company that is capable of giving our students the right input about the industry. Taking into consideration, the fact that at times like these, when recession has taken center stage and your company has stood out and set an example to the faltering companies in the country about how a company must be run.

Request you to kindly grant our CSE students permission to visit your company by the end of this month.

Thanking you,
Principal

'This is the Xerox of the letter you mailed them, if I am not wrong.'

'Yes.'

'You actually typed this and sent it to the company?'

I typed a fake letter with the college header in the name of the Principal; signed and sent it to the company.

'The letter came from the principal's office, Chris.' I grinned. 'And what I just told you now is a LIE.'

'What if the principal actually comes to know about this? Won't he kick you out of our college?'

'Only if he finds out. Prasad has already spoken to the company manager, as one of the college professor, to get the approval.'

'Ok. I did not know that. And what was the reply?'

'He said he will get back to us within a week.'

'Hmmm . . . So they got cheated by the letter?'

'Yes.'

Chapter 12

Gaming

Five days went by and we did not get any intimation from the company manager to whom we had forwarded the letter.

'You think he will reply?'

'Fingers crossed.'

We decided to go and participate in ABC college of Engineering. Actually, it was surprising to know that no one, representing St. Patrick, won in any cultural competition over the past 2 years. The patcult committee resigned to celebrating cultural events in college. People started losing interest in cultural events. Though people liked participating for fun to expand their network, it took a few defeats to understand that losers were not respected in public. The prominent winners in various events in cultural festivals were from Sai Ram College, LSN College and Kali Amman College, while Shruthi and Preethi ensured that SRV College name featured in the list of winners everywhere.

'14 months without a win!' Chris gave a pause. 'You think we will win here?'

'Not sure about you.' I smiled. 'But I am confident my losing streak will end here.' I said. 'I am going to participate in block 'n' tackle. One event that has been recently included in the long list of events in cultural competitions'

'What is block 'n' tackle?'

'An individual will be given a topic like corruption and will be given 2 minutes stage time. The concerned person must talk for and against the topic.'

'The same person?'

'Yes the same person. When the judge says "block", he must support the topic and when the judge exclaims "tackle" he must talk against the topic.'

'Great. So that's an individual event. How about Gaming?'

'Let's see . . . .'

The registrations for the events started and Prasad and Dinesh who accompanied us to the college left immediately to Mayajaal, a multiplex in Chennai. Deepakh promised us that he will join us here, but I knew he was lying and he confirmed it when he put his mobile in switch off mode from the previous night.

'Some sort of team mates you brought along.' It was Chris' idea to bring Dinesh and Prasad, our team mates for Ad-Zap!

'I doubted their credibility when they spoke about that latest Caribbean flick while leaving from college. They had no intentions of coming here, until I said that the multiplex is close by. I promised them free tickets for the evening show if they participate in the event with us. Little did I know that they were addicted to the seas!'

We registered for block 'n' tackle and gaming.

I entered the room to participate in block 'n' tackle and Chris followed to cheer me.

'I thought you also registered.'

'Actually I was planning to participate in the event but look at the competitors.' I saw around and found hardly 5 people seated there in the seats allotted for the participants and over 300 seated in the seats for the audience. As the event was new in the college event list, there are not many who were ready to give a shot in it. 'I see only 5 participants out there.'

'Don't downgrade it to 5. Upgrade it to FIVE!'

I was given the topic outsourcing and when I got on stage, I saw the judge. The judge was a girl who barely 20 years old.

'Do I get any preparation time?'

'You already ran down 10 seconds on the clock.'

'If I you were my girlfriend and if you were in Delhi and I was here, I would ask my friends in Delhi to have an eye on you, so that you do not run away with someone else.'

'Is that the meaning of outsourcing?' She was sensitive and I did not know her name.

'May be! But I have not yet come to my point.'

'You may leave.'

'What the hell? The person who spoke before me said sati is wife killing husband and you let her talk and you stop me now!'

'I am the judge here.'

'Then you must be nuts.' She showed me her middle finger in front of the crowd and disqualified me immediately.

'We can leave for gaming.' I stepped out of the stage and joined Chris, as usual busy in the phone lines with Chitra (I assume).

'Guess our losing streak will continue.' Chris shouted.

'Not when gaming is around.' I exclaimed. With block 'n' tackle, gaming was also introduced in the cultural festivals, proving to the world the impact of gaming in

College students. 80% of the students all around the country voted for gaming in an online poll in Orkut and Facebook. And the games people voted for were Fifa, Counter Strike, Need for speed and World of War craft.

'I think gaming will be tougher than Dumb Charades' Chris thought.

'We will do well.' I believed. 'We should be through to the next round with ease.'

'Okay.'

We were allotted seats in the computer lab, re-modified to look more like a battlefield.

'You can select any team you want.' The game was Fifa.

'Love it. Select Manchester united.' I told Chris. 'They always win.' I looked at the screen and saw the other two guys select Wigan athletic. 'They must be unaware of which team is good or bad.' I leaned towards one of them. 'Select a good team. You don't stand a chance against us with that team.'

'He is a psych.' Chris added, brimming with confidence. 'Give them the score line, buddy.'

'The winner will beat the losers 5-0 minimum.'

'We will see about that.' The person in the opposition team said. I chuckled and whispered 'LOSERS.'

"Fucker pass the ball", "dude move there", "dude block him", "fuck not that pass", "hey, stop him", "hey that's a foul", "shit, he is not letting me go forward", "shit that's a foul", "how did they take the ball?", "that's a crazy tackle."

'BETTER LUCK NEXT TIME.' One of the opposition team members wished me.

'5-0.The match is up.' The host stated.

'Luckily they did not score more.' I told Chris.

'And you told me Manchester united always win.' Chris was angry.

'I was referring to the actual team out there in the real world. This is a game!'

'Shit man. Guess we can never win.'

'I predicted the score right. I think I am seriously a psych!'

'We underestimated the guys when they took Wigan Athletic. That's something we can take back and work on for the future. By the time we become good in the game, they will become legends!'

'Don't be a pessimist, be an optimist.' I wanted to instill the idea of winning into Chris.

'Bro.' Chris put his hand over my shoulder. 'Let me get it straight. Someone told me, "no girls, no power". With us lacking serious talent, we cannot win anything. We were lucky to have team mates who could help us win. But now without them, I don't see us winning today or in the coming future.'

'Believe me dude. Those who face times like these with belief and faith are called men. Once we start winning I don't think there will be any asshole in this world, who can stop us from winning.'

'That's a nice line.'

I smiled. 'Inspired?'

'Not a bit.' Chris said.

'So what are we going to do now?'

'I heard that chick looks sexy as a pirate in the movie. I don't want to miss it.'

'And I heard her boyfriend kills the captain of a ship and becomes the captain of the ship and lives in the sea forever.'

'You are spoiling it for me.'

'Thanks.'

'Anyways I am checking it for sure. I will go with my friend and that friend is not you.'

'Oh'

'And one more thing'

'Go on'

'I had my thinking cap on for some time and I have finally decided to take this decision.'

'Never knew you had a thinking cap'

'I am not going to participate again in any of the competitions coming up. Sorry Justin, you are on your own from today.'

'You have put a smile on my face.'

'Believe me. I am a man of my word.' Chris assured me. 'I don't think we will ever win.'

*　　*　　*

December 2007:

'So this is Chitra.' We were seated in Coffee day. Chris finally introduced Chitra to me. She looked sweet and innocent, not how I had expected her to be. 'And she is your girlfriend.'

'Right' Chris politely said. Deepakh kept staring at her. 'Order whatever you want.' He said rudely to Deepakh to distract him. 'The treat is on me.'

'Thanks' Deepakh smiled. 'You look nice madam.' He said, as I fell down laughing.

'Call me Chitra.' Suggested Chitra, quite embarrassed after Deepakh called her _madam._

'Ok madam.' He said again. 'I always wanted to have a girlfriend like you madam. But sadly I could not find any.' Chris boiled with anger.

'I wanted you to confess.' I interrupted Deepakh and said to Chris. 'That she was your girlfriend and it took me 2 and a half years in making you do it.' Chris nodded.

'You mean to say he did not inform you that I was his girlfriend?' Chitra had a pleasant tone. She was a second year student in MOP College, Chennai, pursuing her B.Com there.

'I knew nothing about your relationship a month ago.'

'Though you guys were in the same class for two years?'

'We also stay in the same apartment!'

'That's bad. I thought class mates share everything that happens between them and their girlfriends. Isn't that the reason why friends are for?' Chitra looked disappointed.

'You want me to request them to decrease the A/c temperature down to 18? It quite hot out here.' I asked Chris, who seriously felt the heat of Chitra.

'No issues.' Chitra smiled. She was close to 5 feet 5 inch tall and was thin. She seemed to have complete control over her eating habits. She wore a salwar kameez for the occasion and Chris informed me that that was her usual attire.

She suddenly turned to the nearby table and screamed 'Babbbyyyyyy.' She made some funny faces and weird sounds.

"Coochie coo, choo choo chooo . . ." She went on . . .

A family was seated next to our table and they had their baby seated in a chair facing Chitra.

'So sweet' Chitra said 'I want to have a baby like that.' I said nothing.

'You must get married to have babies, Chitra.' Chris whispered.

'Then please marry me.' Chitra pleaded. 'Then I can have lots of kids.' She smiled.

'It's not as simple as you think it is.'

'But I want to have one.' Chitra said. 'Won't you marry me?'

'Of course, yes' Chris assured.

'Give it in writing.' Deepakh and I chuckled.

'I can give it in writing.' Deepakh stated. 'In blood'

'Shut up' I whispered to Deepakh.

'My mother told me never to hide my emotions. It is not good for health.' Deepakh said, as Chitra silently giggled, clearly indicating that she was impressed.

'Not now.' Chris said.

'Let's talk about something else.' I smiled. 'So what are you having?'

'Anything that tastes good.' Chitra shifted her focus to our table

I paused for a moment. 'You sound like you have never been to this place before.'

'That's true.' She smiled. 'Chris takes me only to vegetarian restaurants and buys me dosa, idly and vadai.'

'Whoa!' I stared at Chris for a moment. 'Dosa, idly and vadai!' I smiled. 'And he tells his grandparents that he goes out to teach computer applications to his school mate in some other college at night on weekdays.'

'He does teach me a lot on weekdays.' Chitra chuckled.

'And what about regular weekends? Neither does he stay back at home nor does he come out with me? You volunteer in some blood camp, don't you?'

'Yes! I am part of an organization that collects blood from donors and donates it to the needy. Chris is a regular donor. He's so sweet.'

'I am also sweet and I am also ready to donate my blood.' Deepakh pleaded.

'I get it.' I smiled. Deepakh had fallen for her. Hmmm! Fallen for Chris' girl! *A good talking point!*

'You did not tell him, did you?' She asked Chris. 'So I guess he did not tell you that we are going to Sangeetha restaurant after this.' She was smiling. 'I think you must invite your friend too.' She looked at Chris.

'Not needed.'

'I think we should take them with us.' Chitra smiled.

'No I have some work today. So I will not be able to join you guys.' I replied.

'Take me with you.' Deepakh pleaded like a mad man. 'I will follow you wherever you. *You and me, in this beautiful world!*' He sang

Chitra smiled. She was surprising impressed by Deepakh, but not Chris, who was raging with anger. 'So what do you guys actually discuss about?'

'Some random stuff'

'Like?'

'Random. Anything that comes to our mind at that moment'

'Chris told me he talks only about me.' Chitra asked anxiously. 'Does he?'

'Ah . . .' Chris almost looked like he'd fall on my feet, as I replied. 'I meant only I talk about random things. He tells me all the good things in the world about you. He loves you so much!'

Did you have to lie to her about that, when you actually have heard Chris mentioning Chitra's name only twice? A friend in need is a friend indeed!

Chitra smiled. 'Did he tell you that he goes to the temple near his place and feeds the beggars every Friday because I asked him to?' She asked.

'He did.' I was controlling my laughter.

'And you know, Chris told me that he does not look at any girl other than me.' Chitra stated proudly.

'Hmmm . . .' I thought deeply.

'Hmmm means yes right?' She seemed worried.

'Yes.'

'Good.' She sighed in relief.

'I can guarantee you that I will not even look at my mother from today.' Deepakh added.

'Shut up dude!' I blasted Deepakh. 'That sounds cheap.'

'What's cheap about that?' Deepakh defended himself.

"Aaja aaja" my mobile sang. 'Excuse me.'

'Sure!' Chris said happily.

I walked out and attended the call. It was Prasad. 'What happened?'

'They are not interested.'

'You must be joking. I am not talking about Microsoft or Google. It is Futura technologies for God's sake.'

'Believe me. They think they are one of the former.'

'Fuck them.'

'I know.' Prasad was disappointed. 'What do we do now?'

'Is Param there?'

'Why do you ask?'

'Because he is your bloody roommate'

'He is online now.'

'Give him the phone.'

'Now?'

'Now'

'Hi.' Param said. 'What do you want from me?'

'Possible to meet you today?'

'I am free 30 minutes from now. Can you make it?'

'Betting?'

'Good. See you soon.' I switched off the mobile and went back to the table.

'Sorry guys. Have some urgent work. I have to leave NOW!' I pulled Deepakh from his place.

'You can have your cup of coffee and then leave right?' Chitra asked me as I found it hard to pull Deepakh out of his place.

'Some other day' I answered. 'Thanks and good meeting you.'

'Ok good for us' Chitra smiled. 'We were anyways discussing serious things and needed Deepakh to leave the scene.'

'But I don't want to.' Cried Deepakh

'Ok.' I smiled, and forced Deepakh out of his place and started walking with him. 'See you guys later.'

'When?' Chitra asked.

'He said later.' Chris was interested in safeguarding her from Deepakh.

'We should plan these meetings more often.' She said.

'Ya sure'

'And don't bother about Chris. He told me he is available any time any day for me.' Chitra smiled.

'Any time eh?' I chuckled.

'That's what boyfriends are for.' She grinned. 'By the way you guys go for cultural programs, right? Chris has spoken a lot about it.'

'Yes. It is fun.'

'Count me in the next time you guys go out for any show. Chris does not take me to any of the colleges he participates in. I am counting on you to take me.'

'Leave Justin out of this. I will let you know the next time we go and take you with us.' Chris replied.

'I will take you.' Deepakh roared. 'I will take the angel anywhere she wants to.'

'Suits me.' Chitra smiled. 'Should I hug Justin and Deepakh since he is leaving?'

'Not needed. We are not in US or UK to do that.'

'But we talk in English!'

'Justin, please leave.' Chris caught Chitra so that she could not get up from her place and do what was running in her mind.

'Fine' I smiled as Deepakh continuously tried to get back to the table and finally succumbed to my pressure.

*   *   *

'What is he doing?' Param asked Prasad.

'Typing'

Param paused for a second and stared at Prasad. 'I know that dog. What is he typing?'

'He will be done in a few moments.' Deepakh looked dejected in the corner. 'Why is that guy seated like that?'

'Who knows? Did some close friend of yours die bro?' Param asked Deepakh.

'I have a broken heart.' Deepakh cried.

'Do you want fevicol to stick it?' Prasad chuckled.

'Not funny.'

'I did not say it was a joke.' Prasad replied back.

'Ok.' Param came closer to me. 'Looks like a letter.'

'Of course it is a letter.' Prasad interrupted.

'I know that. But why is he typing a letter in our room?'

'God knows. May be his system is not working . . .'

'I won't travel 15kms from my house just to type "just another letter" in your room.' I replied.

'That makes sense too.' Prasad stated.

'Yes it makes sense.' Param said.

'Is it a love letter?' Prasad asked. They stayed in the rented room, which looked more like a breeding place for rats.

'Why do you say that?' I asked.

'Because you cannot type a love letter in your house, can you?' Param replied.

'Makes sense' Prasad agreed.

'But to who is it addressed?'

'To the director'

'Director?'

'Don't mistake me. This is not a love letter. This is an official letter from a manager to our college principal.'

'But you are the one typing it? I'm confused.'

'I am done.'

'Can we read?'

'Of course!' I moved away from the computer.

'Thanks.'

'Keep the thanks after reading it'

'Ok'

FUTURA TECHNOLOGIES

From,
The Manager,
Futura technologies,
Bangalore.
To,
The director,
St. Patrick College of Engineering,
Chennai.

Respected sir,

I would like the CSE 2005-09 batch of your college to come to our campus for an industrial visit in the coming month. We have shortlisted your college as the only college which has the right students to visit our prestigious campus. Please accept this proposal and send them to Bangalore as quickly as possible. And ensure that they stay here for a full day, so that they can be given the complete KT needed to understand the system.

Thanking You,
Manager.

Please contact me on 7100024567 for any queries and let me know when you are sending your students.

'That's my mobile number!' Param said.

'I know.' I smiled. 'Use it for this occasion.'

'Great.' Param laughed. 'The staff and the manager live under the same roof. You think I will blow up my college life for some shit industrial visit?'

'You already have 15 arrears.' I reminded him. 'That makes you eligible for a person who has already blown up.'

'He has a point.' Prasad agreed.

'I know.' Param remembered. 'So what's the worst that can happen? Semester drop?'

'That's the worst.' I encouraged him. 'At least you will have a reason to give to your parents if you fail this time around.'

'Some friend you are turning out to be.' Param said. 'A cunning fox you are! People encourage their friends to study and pass, and here you are, giving me reasons to celebrate failure. No wonder Jeffrey told me not to rub shoulders with you. He said you stink in nature.'

'I am doing this for the class.' I smiled. 'Not for me.'

'That's valid. So you must become the martyr, not me. It's like you are planning to kill and I am going forward for executing it.'

'A hit man'

'Thanks. At least they are paid and have a name. What do I get? I will take the risk and you will become the hero if it clicks?'

'Never knew you were such a sissy.' I knew his weak point. 'When you spoke in front of the class, I thought you are a man of your word. But now you sound as good as a chicken. You are no different from the thousands who go unnoticed in this world.'

'I am not a sissy.'

'You sound like one. I thought you will take this opportunity and do this for the class. You are one of the best in talking in different voices.' I kept inspiring him

'Mimicry'

'You can never become a great movie maker if you stay like this.'

'Yes'

'Yes. You are the best and I came to you. Leave it. You cannot be like Prasad. I am just surprised that a sissy is a daredevil's roommate.'

'Yeah, I'm a daredevil.' Prasad raised his collar in pride.

'I am not scared. I just think twice before doing something.'

'If you think twice, you will do nothing.'

'Believe me, I don't think even once.' Prasad smiled.

'Good.' I teased Prasad. 'Do you think before drinking?'

'No.'

'Before watching porn?'

'No.'

'Before masturbating.'

'No.'

'Before falling in love?' Deepakh questioned from nowhere.

'Never.' Param thought. 'You are right. Why am I wasting my time thinking?'

Thank God, I have dumb friends here. I smiled.

'Dude you opened my eyes.' He kept his hands over my shoulders. 'I am the manager now. So what do I do now?'

'What do managers do?'

'You gave me the post. You tell me.'

'Nothing. Just attend the calls you get and be believable.'

'I will try to.'

'Hope the professors and the principal fall for our trap.'

'Hope Chitra falls for me.' Deepakh stated and no one replied. *He was in love!*

'It will work out well don't worry. What happened when the Portuguese under Vasco Da Gama first landed in India?' I asked Param and Prasad.

'We invited them wholeheartedly.' Param said.

'That's what Indians do.' I gave a cunning smile. 'We invite danger wholeheartedly.'

'Hmm . . . very true.' Prasad said. 'But thanks to them, English followed them.' He gleamed.

'They made us their slaves, fucker. Why are you thanking them?' Param asked Prasad angrily.

'Dude my girlfriend is an Anglo-Indian.'

'Ah . . .' I smiled.

'She would have been sleeping with an English guy now, if her ancestors did not set foot in our country and stayed back to control us.'

'Hmmm . . .'

Chapter 13

A winner is born

'How in the world did you fall for her?' I asked Deepakh.

'That's love I suppose.' He smiled.

'That's true.' I said and turned to Chris. 'But what the fuck are you doing out here, Chris?'

'That's what I am asking myself.' Chris paused for a moment. 'What am I doing here?' Chris said. 'And how the fuck can you fall for my girlfriend!'

'I am a free bird. I can select anyone I want to love.' Deepakh said boldly. Honestly speaking, Deepakh had really gone nuts about Chitra. He had been torturing Chris and me for Chitra's number and in spite of Chitra rejecting his friend request in Facebook over a hundred times, he kept adding her again and again. *Same story as Zuckerberg!*

'That does not allow you to love my babe.' Chris said.

'Yudhisthira, Bhima, Arjuna, Nakula and Sahadeva were the pandavas who married one woman, Draupadi.

135

Here you and I are just two. So there is still space for 3 more.' Deepakh said happily.

'He is gone.' I informed Chris as Deepakh. 'As expected, you did follow me. You could not stay back in class with the thought that I'd be having fun at cultural, could you?' I asked. 'Now you must accept the fact that you are not a man of your word.'

We had just got into the college premises of Madras Institute of Technology Chrompet, Chennai, one of the premier engineering institutes in Chennai. Surprisingly they did not have dumb charades or Ad-Zap lined up during the fest; and so had no choice but to register for JAM.

JAM was loosely based on "group discussion", the only major difference being JAM (Just a minute) had all informal topics brought to the discussion room. Each group had 5 to 10 participants and a topic would be put forward by the host in the discussion room. Anyone can take up the initiative and start speaking. The others were allowed to interrupt the speaker only if the speaker made mistakes like "repeating points", "grammatical errors", "jumping the gun", "time wasting tactics", "out of context" etc.

The participant who spots the right error gets the opportunity to take off from where the other speaker stopped. Participants hardly spoke for 2 to 3 seconds in a closely fought out JAM event, as a common man in India made a million errors in one single English sentence, knowingly or unknowingly. People pointing out a lot of wrong errors, gained negative points and those who spoke lot of crap, also ended up getting the same. So in simple terms, it was better to stay numb than to talk!

'The event starts exactly at 4pm. That is almost 7 hours from now.' The college president informed me, Deepakh and Chris.

'You must be joking.' Chris stated.

'I am not smiling.' The president replied.

'Call up Chitra; I want to listen to her voice.' Deepakh stated.

'Fuck.' Chris said. 'I should have stayed back at home. Today is a holiday and I am wasting it out here with you two.'

'What would have you done back home?' I asked.

'I would have . . . hmmm' Chris thought. 'Let me think.'

'I know. You would have been on the phone with Chitra, praising her.' I said.

'That's right.' Chris said. 'Don't share your views about Chitra with any of your friends.'

'I won't'

'Share it with me, please.' Deepakh begged.

7 hours with Chris and a now mad in love Deepakh in that auditorium? I would rather go back home and sleep.

'We can chat.' Chris said.

'About what?' I asked. 'Chitra?'

'I prefer that.' Deepakh exclaimed. 'Let's talk about her.'

Chris came close to my ears. 'Because of this nut, I am not able to call her nowadays. He is killing me.'

'He is dying of love.' I chuckled.

'No.' Chris stated to Deepakh. 'Anything random man . . . other than Chitra!'

'Ok.' I concluded. MIT was not as crowded as Iron College. 'What's special today?'

'There is a cultural festival in Muthu College and Aalim College also today.'

'Those colleges are situated almost 50 kilometers from the city!'

'And the trains that left to Chengalpattu were full in the morning.'

'AC and MC are located far away from the city!'

'Yes.' Chris stated. 'And you know what; Param informed me that *the terror gang* has left to Muthu College today morning.'

'Man. No wonder the book told aim big. People go in thousands to public toilets when the clean private ones are empty.'

'Nice way to compare a college.' Chris smiled.

'Oh' I said. 'And some inside news for you: those guys *(terror gang)* drink!'

'Hmmm . . .' Chris said. 'What's so inside about that?'

'I thought drinking was something that people don't do at our age.' I said.

'Have you ever visited a tasmac?' Chris asked me.

'No man.'

'If you do get a chance please, do so. People of our age flood Tasmac, because of love.' Chris informed. 'We account to 40% of the customers. 30% people working in MNCs. What comes by spending hours in A/C rooms is vomited in Tasmac shops.'

'Hmmm . . .' Deepakh joined us 'Cause people joining MNCs are mostly people who were like us a few years back.'

'Is data right?'

'Right' Chris smiled. 'Let's go for a walk.' He said, pulling me and Deepakh out. 'Let's spend some time WALKING.'

'Hmm . . . look at that movie poster out there' I said. We got out of the college and looked across the road outside the college premises. 'They are playing *Love Tonight.*'

'Sounds adult' Deepakh smiled. 'And someone told me they have to pay extra tax if the movie in regional language is titled in English.'

'I don't think that rule is applicable for adult films.' I guessed.

'Yeah I guess'

We walked across to the theatre, named "Good Theatre". It was a small theatre that usually only screened 'A' rated movies. *A Decent name for an indecent theater*

'The sign board below states "*only ages 18 and above*" Chris said.

'We are adults.' I reminded Chris. 'And so are eligible to see (A) movies. And luckily it starts in 10 minutes from now. So we can burn 3 hours in this theater.'

'Hmmm . . . valid'

'I can hardly see anyone standing in the ticket counter. Guess people are bankrupt.'

'Recession' Deepakh politely added.

'Yes. And it is the last week of this month. Understandably almost all the marvadi pockets will be filled with money.' I said.

'Yes. High interest rates' Chris smiled.

'How are the marvadi's pockets filled to the brim when ours are empty?' Deepakh asked.

'Simple, they work to give and we plan to spend.' Chris stated.

'Three tickets' I smiled.

'Rs.60.' the guy in the ticket counter said.

'For one?'

'Three.'

'Ok.'

'Show me your college ID cards.'

'Why do you need that?'

'I want to confirm that you three are adults.'

'Ok. Here you go.'

Chris came close to the counter. 'How many scenes does the movie have?'

He handed the tickets to me. '69.'

'Not that. I am referring to those scenes. The actual stuff?'

'I must say you will NOT be disappointed!' The guy smiled.

'You sure it is safe to watch a flick here.' Deepakh whispered in my ears.

'As safe as in the hands of the transporter' I assured.

'Wherever the transporter went, danger followed.' Deepakh cried.

'Just get in and enjoy the show.' I pushed him in.

* * *

'Dude the girl is going close to the guy. I think the time has come.'

'Yes. I've never seen a movie of this genre in a silver screen.'

'Whoa! She is taking so much time to remove her hair clip. This is time wasting tactics.'

'They are keeping the audience on the edge man.'

'What will she remove next?'

'Wait. I hope it is her shirt. She looks good.'

Chris did not reply. The music was romantic and the director focused on the ceiling fan.

'She is now removing her eye lens! Fuck.'

'This is outrageous. She is taking 10 minutes to remove it. When are they going to show the actual picture?'

'You know what. The rest of the people in the theater have gone out for a smoke.'

'Thambi. She will remove her chain next, then her shoes, then her earnings, her watch, her rings and then her bangles. That will take about 20 minutes. So you guys can actually go out and have something.' The guy sitting next to Chris informed us as he was getting up from his seat.

'Oh . . . What happens next?' Chris asked angrily.

'The guy will remove his watch, chain, rings, shoes, socks, his spectacles for the next 15 minutes.'

'Oh . . . You've already seen this movie?' Deepakh asked. He was restless from the time we got into the cinema hall.

'Yes.'

'So when will the actual scene come?'

'After 35 minutes of this outrageous nonsense, there is a song that runs for 5 minutes. Then they will pan the camera and cover the entire house 360 degrees for about 15 minutes, with the audio of the girl moaning and finally the scene will be complete.'

Chris and I stared at each other in disgust, as Deepakh hid his face with his hand. 'So why did you come back again?'

'This time I'm going to concentrate closely when the camera pans, to see if I can watch anything interesting. I hope to peek through the window to see what is happening inside. I did not concentrate last time. This time I am well prepared.'

Asshole! I thought to myself 'All the best' I wished him as he left the theater.

'We could have rented a CD at home. CDs are fool proof. No wonder CDs are popular.' Chris cried.

'So how did this movie get an adult certificate? Even kids have nothing to see in this.' I said.

'I think this has to do with the censor board of India. They are very clear on not showing sexual scenes on public screens.'

They are the ones who censored the sexual positions book too I thought for a moment. 'We got cheated by the movie name.'

'The actual scene will be available in CD man.' Chris reminded. 'So I am not complaining a lot.'

'I will not spend more for this crap!'

*   *   *

The movie ended at 1:15 PM, giving us enough time to have lunch and join the competitors on stage for JAM at 3:45 PM.

'I had a good nap! The A/C effects in the theater were seriously good.'

'Yes. At least we got our money's worth.' Deepakh smiled. 'You know, God stopped us from seeing bad things on screen. I believe it was God who censored this movie, not the censor board.'

'Don't tell me God works only in Cinema hall, cause almost everyone, including myself and Chris, see porn once in a while. He does not seem interested in censoring online!'

Deepakh thought for a moment. 'He does not run a censor company.'

The event started at 4:05 PM and surprisingly there were only 8 participants.

'So much for the *big* college tag!' I whispered to Chris. 'You think the participants will join us shortly?'

'If only someone was there to inform those assholes in Muthu College.' Chris switched off his mobile.

'As the number of participants is way less than expected, we will just have one round and that will be the finals.' The host informed us.

'Direct finals' Chris and I smiled in joy. 'Finally we made it to the next stage.' Deepakh was sitting silently. 'Dude you can also give a shot, because you never know: today might be your day!'

'As you have forced me to . . .' Deepakh stated.

'I am not forcing you to'

'No you will' Deepakh said 'I will take part.'

'Ok' I was filled with joy. 'We are going home with some certificates for sure.' So it became 9.

We got on stage and stood silently. 'Your 1st topic is *0 and 1 are binary numbers.*' The judge looked like a decent and an equally polite dude, as he immediately allowed Deepakh participate in the event. 'Please introduce yourself.'

'Hanna from Women's Christian college!' She immediately caught my attention. My eyes followed her from the moment I got on stage.

'Karthik from Bhargav University.' Fat boy.

'Chris from St. Patrick College.'

'Justin from the same college.'

'Deepakh also from St. Patrick College.'

'Abi from Radha College.' He was a tall guy.

'And what about you three?' The host asked three guys standing numb.

'What is this competition we are participating in?' One of them asked.

'Ok. We will have the finals with just 6 participants.' The host smiled.

'Make it 5.' Chris moved out of the stage.

'What happened?' I was surprised.

'I will puke if I stay there longer. You know I vomited when I was told to take a seminar during the database class in college.'

'Ah . . . Stage fear.' I stated. 'But you had none when we participated in LSN?'

'We had chicks there'

'Great.' The host was not surprised. 'You guys may now begin.'

'I know that 0 blah . . . . blah . . . . 1 . . . . blah' Hanna's mouth was an express train that never reached its destination and incidentally she was standing next to me. All that I could do was watch her talk. She was dressed in a white sleeveless t-shirt and black jeans. She wore spectacles and was very fair. I was speechless, not only because she was next to me, but also because she did not give the rest of us a chance to talk.

'If you want to oppose to what she is saying BARK.' The host ordered.

'Bow Bow.' That was a surprise as Deepakh barked. 'Time wasting tactics.'

'Right.' Judge agreed.

'0 and 1 blah blah blah' Now he spoke more. Abi and Karthik left the stage as I stared at Hanna and Deepakh fight it out.

I looked down at Chris who pointed to me the stairs that would help me get out of the stage. But sadly I was stuck to my place and I was left in a trance, not knowing what to do. I was numb struck. A girl and boy BARKING and shouting out English words was all that I heard. I did not understand a thing neither did I contribute. And the guy barking was none other than the guy I knew personally and who spent days and months with Chris and me outside the college classroom. *Where had he been hiding this talent for so long?*

'Don't you have anything to talk?' The host asked me.

'How can I?'

He smiled. The event went on for over 20 minutes and I watched Hanna and Deepakh fight it out.

'Good show!' The host said and applauded the three of us on stage.

Chris pulled me out of the stage and made me sit next to him. 'I think Deepakh won it!' I said. 'Hanna did not smile at the host. She is probably second.' Deepakh stood next to the host and did not come next to me.

'And you?' Chris asked me.

'Me? Dead!'

After a while, the judge had made his decision. 'The results are . . .' The host began.

I was confident on who'd win. First to Deepakh and second to Hanna

'1st and the 2nd place goes to St. Patrick college.' The host concluded. 'That is Deepakh 1st, Justin 2nd.'

Results are never a reflection of what happens on stage.

What the hell. The girl was stunned. 'Deepakh scored 5; Justin scored a 0, Hanna a—2.' The host smiled.

'Fuck.' Chris said as I sank into my seat. 'That's a double fuck!'

'Congrats!' The host shook hands with us.

'The girl deserved it.' I told him.

'Not as per the results. She spoke a lot and earned a lot of negatives. You kept your mouth shut, which is one of the best strategies to win in JAM.'

'He is right.' Hanna came to me. She was ready to go down in tears but she cleverly hid it behind her spectacles. 'You deserved it. I spoke too much.' She said.

A girl who wanted to win decently! Hope Shruthi and Preethi meet this girl. They have a lesson or two to learn from Hanna.

*   *   *

I won my first (legal) winning certificate and 500 bucks. And that too without murmuring a word! *How cruel can life be!*

'The book said *Keep your mouth shut when it matters the most.*'

'Which book?' Chris said, as Deepakh walked silently next to him with his winning certificate and 1000 bucks.

'The book we bought in the book fair. That book.'

'Oh' Chris felt out of place, as he was the only person who walked empty handed. 'You still remember the chapters, do you?'

'Yes. It was one of the few books that I have ever read in my life.' I smiled. 'For this one reason I would say, my investment was not wasted. Implementing what I learnt from the book has helped me bag 500 bucks. So 450 bucks profit.'

'I don't think what you did out there was intentional.' Chris said. He looked at the certificate with jealousy. 'If I would have participated, you would have had to share that money that you are presently carrying in your previously thin pocket!'

'500 bucks is good. I will treat you.' I smiled. 'And how about you, Deepakh?'

'I some debts that I need to clear. So no treat from my side.' Deepakh stated.

'But a winning certificate man!' Chris said 'You finally did it.' He looked at Deepakh. 'Where were you hiding for so long?'

'Nowhere' He smiled 'Chitra gave me the energy to talk'

'She has made a change in my life too!' Chris said.

'Yes. Hope this is the first of many to come.' We were standing in the station and talking, when I saw Hanna come and stand right next to us.

'You think she is mallu?' Chris asked me.

'I think yes.' I said smiling. 'Today is my lucky day.' I chuckled. 'But something tells me it is going to get better.' Hanna turned and saw me. Surprisingly she smiled.

'I know it is disheartening.' I walked closer to her and started.

'Don't worry. This is not the first time I have come across a defeat in this manner. It hardly has any impact on me.'

'Oh . . . that's great! So do you participate in these competitions regularly?'

'If there is JAM or debate, yes!' She smiled.

'Ok.'

'I missed a trick out there.' She seemed interested in a conversation. 'Your friend spoke really well.' She said as Deepakh walked in.

'I agree.' I actually did not agree. I wanted her to talk about me, but there she was, appreciating Deepakh.

'Yes. But I spoke too much.' Chris picked up his mobile and moved out of the scene. 'I should have had control.' Deepakh smiled. 'How did you talk that well? As in, I have never seen you participate anywhere. Do you go to only the IITs and the universities in Bangalore? It comes to me as a surprise to see people like you hidden from the cultural world for so long.'

'It happens.' Deepakh said.

'Deepakh is participating for the first time in a cultural event, EVER!' I interrupted her. 'Even I have not seen you anywhere.'

'That's because I have been participated in only 5 cultural competitions here in Chennai.'

'Oh'

'I usually represent the country in other country cultural and debate festivals.'

I shut my mouth. 'You must seriously apply for the AICC. I think you might make it.' She said to Deepakh. I thought for a moment: We could not even make it to the patcult committee in College, and there she was, asking Deepakh to enroll for AICC (All India Cultural Committee)

'Surely'

'Your friend was pathetic.' She said pointing to me. 'Not worth the money he got. He must feel insulted to tell others that he won the way he did today.'

'Something tells me these 500 bucks are yours. I totally am undeserving of this.'

'No no. You deserve it for standing numb for 20 minutes.' She said. 'That in itself is an achievement. I have never seen people become stones on stage.'

'That's sounds like an insult.'

'I suppose it is.' She smiled. She sounded friendly, not to me, but to Deepakh. 'Hope to beat you next time.' She challenged.

'My pleasure'

'Are we going to get in?' Chris came back to the scene, as the train neared the station.

'What happened?' I asked.

'Chitra's number is engaged.' Chris said disappointedly. 'Today is not a lucky day for me.'

Hanna got in and I quickly got in behind her. 'This is the ladies' compartment.' She informed.

'Oh.' I jumped out of the compartment, before anyone could forcefully push me out. 'Where are you going to get down?'

'Why do you ask that?'

'It won't harm you if you tell me.'

'Nungambakkam' she said. 'Bye Deepakh.'

I got into the general compartment with Chris and a blushing Deepakh.

'You did not get her number?' Chris asked Deepakh.

'I don't want her number. I want Chitra's.' He said.

I said nothing. She clearly avoided me and despised me. Why not? I ruined her day, by standing numb. *How cruel is life? I want to talk with Hanna and she converses with Deepakh, and Deepakh wants to talk with Chitra and she is in love with Chris!*

But I must confess: she seriously grabbed my attention.

'We can get it once we get down in Nungambakkam.' I said.

'But we must get down in Guindy?' Chris asked.

'Not today.' I smiled.

*   *   *

'Dude she is not here.' I searched inside the coach and all around me in the station.

'Justin, you are such an asshole. Girls never tell the truth and surely not to random strangers! I would have been surprised if she'd spoken the truth. Good, at least she proved that she is a girl.'

'But she was different.'

'Oh . . . love huh?'

'No . . . I wouldn't say that blindly. She had something that I liked.'

'But she did not like you.' Deepakh exclaimed proudly. 'Not a bit.'

'That's something special with the girls of our generation. Good or bad, their assets are worth commenting.' Chris chuckled.

Ping I received a message.

It is me, Prasad. The College is taking us to Bangalore.

'Whoa!' I showed it to Chris. 'Mark this day in the calendar. This day rocks!'

Chapter 14

The trip that mattered

'Dude, kiss me!' Prasad came close to Chris.

'What?' Chris moved away.

'Make my lips wet. Don't be shy!'

'Asshole' Chris jumped away. 'This guy is totally out of his senses.' Chris complained. 'At least if Eliza had asked me, I would have accepted.'

'She looks bad.' I reminded him.

'Good enough for our class.' He said quickly.

I saw Arun S silently come close to Chris. 'Mushrooms are taking control of Prasad, man. And I thought the trip will be fun.'

'Who said it is not?' Jerome was seated in the front row. 'We are having bloody fun.'

'Hmm . . . drinking and smoking and drugs' I said to Chris. 'Surprising these things seem fun to them.'

Prasad kissed Chris quickly and gave a devilish smile. 'I did it.'

150

'Shit! You fucker' Chris said, as I roared out in laughter.

'I took a photo of that.' Deepakh said. 'I can show it to Prasad and Chris' girlfriends. They will look for replacements.' He was referring to himself. 'You know, there are a lot of guys in the waiting list.'

'Trip is awesome.' Jeffrey came and sat next to us. 'Finally you did something good.'

'A compliment from my foe!' I smiled. 'So that means I am now part of the class?'

'Of course, yes.' Jeffrey said. I was very surprised with the way Jeffrey interacted with me. He looked like the Jeffrey I knew in 11th grade. 'And you know what; I have already informed the staffs in our department that you cheated them with a fake letter. Actually I gave them a written statement about everything you did when we crossed Tamil Nadu border. They will be waiting to greet you there, once we reach Chennai again.'

I sat silently for a moment and then quickly pounded on Jeffrey with anger, pushing him down and gave him a strong blow in his face. 'Bloody fucking bastard!' I roared.

'You fucker' Jeffrey hit back.

'Are you human?' I roared. 'Good for nothing asshole' I shouted out.

'Ha ha! I don't give a damn about what you say. You are on the losing side.'

'I did this for you guys.' I said to everyone in the bus. 'This guy has always been working against me.' I got up and roared. 'He heads the cultural committee and goes everywhere and does not even participate. Sits pretty in class, does nothing and calls himself head.'

'You are no better than me.' Jeffrey also got up. 'Catches a girl's dupatta and wins. You have no right to talk against me.'

'I won one on my own.' I shouted back.

'And that too without delivering a single dialogue or a word!' Roared Chris out of nowhere. All paused for a moment as Chris came to me and murmured. 'How was it?'

'It did not help.'

'Ah! There you have it.' Jeffrey said to a silent crowd. The staff in the bus instructed the driver to park the bus until the fight ended.

'But he did it for us.' Arun S shouted. 'Not for himself.'

'One good grammatically correct sentence from Arun' Chris whispered as everyone agreed to Arun S.

'I accept' Param added as everyone agreed. 'Jeffrey fucker, you have lost the respect that we had for you. If Justin gets screwed, so will you.'

Jerome went close to Jeffrey and whispered some words. Jeffrey clearly realized that for the first time in his life, the class stood against him. Jeffrey said nothing and took his seat in the bus.

'Thanks.' I finally felt like I was wanted by my class mates, when Chacko slowly came to me and told

'Jeffrey was joking.' I was shocked to hear that. 'But I would say he was planning to do the same once we reached College.' He paused and continued. 'He won't do that, now that he has clearly realized that the class will support you with respect to this context.'

'Looks like people will work for a better tomorrow.' Chris informed me.

'That sounds copied.' Deepakh noted Chris' statement.

I said nothing and sat silent.

*   *   *

'I thought this was supposed to be an Industrial Visit!' Balaji said. 'Are we seriously going to the company?'

'Believe me.' Chris smiled. 'We will learn a lot.'

'Ok.' Balaji smiled. 'I will take my notes and keep it ready.'

'What will he learn?' Chris asked me, recovering from the kiss Prasad gave.

'Bull shit.' I finally laughed. Jeffrey and his terror gang sat silently in front without murmuring a word. Jeffrey knew he had jumped the gun and before he could make it worse, Jerome forced him to leave the scene.

'Better we be reaching before 6 in the evening. I want to going number one badly.' I knew it was Arun S.

'He talks like he is actually peeing now.' Chris roared so loud that Arun S turned back and stared at him. 'Don't look at me like that. I am scared.' I laughed with him.

'Lousy people' Arun S said helplessly.

*　　*　　*

'What? The company is closed!' Sighed Professor Samuel, who took Data Structures for us. He accompanied us to Bangalore.

We were standing outside the company. Samuel was a polite guy and if not for him, Jeffrey and I would have been standing in some local bus stop, waiting to catch a bus back to college. And that was simply because he did not know what the fight was for and was simply unaware of my gag! 'The manager said they work on Saturday.'

'I am not feeling well.' Param announced.

'Go do it somewhere in the street.' I informed. Param quickly moved away from the bus and stood there.

'I think I will call the manager.' The professor dialed the number.

'Hello Sir. This is Samuel Dass from St. Patrick Engineering College. My students and I are standing outside your company's gate. We are here for the industrial visit . . .' he continued.

I could see Param from far on the phone pretending to be the manager, trying to handle this situation. It was too funny to see my professor sweat in tension, as Param gave shitty reasons.

'Oh . . . ok. Ok Sir.' The staff said and switched off his mobile. 'It seems the company had an emergency call for maintenance and had to shut the office. He apologized profusely.'

The professor actually bought this crap.

Balaji took his book and went to the watchman who did not let us in. 'So do we need to get a knowledge transfer from the watchman?'

'If he is a computer graduate, he will help you with your doubts. But he is a watchman! So I guess he will give you a KT on who goes in and who comes out, and about his duty timings.'

'But he is working for this company and he would have witnessed a lot of things.' Balaji said. 'I'm sure he would have learnt something.'

'Oh really? Come let's ask him what he thinks of C' Chris pulled Balaji and took him to the watchman.

'Watchman Anna, what do you think of C?' Chris asked the watchman in Tamil. Many people in Bangalore knew Tamil.

'No sea in Bangalore. Go back to Tamil Nadu.' He replied back.

'There you go with his knowledge on computers. Idiot' Chris scoffed at Balaji.

Balaji accepted defeat and moved back.

Many vomited in front of the company because of the excessive booze they consumed and others because of the bus travel.

'10k wasted.' Cried Prasad as he vomited everything he consumed.

'That's a gift from us to you.' Chris told the watchman. '10k worth of shit directly from the mouth'

'What did the manager say?' Param came back to the scene.

'Shut up!' I silenced him.

'Okay'

'I think I will call him and ask if we can visit the company on Monday. Maybe we can seek permission and stay here.' Samuel redialed the manager's number. Param's pocket vibrated incessantly. 'He is not picking up the mobile.'

How will he? I was tensed. *When he is standing right next to you?*

'He might not be interested in taking us in on Monday.'

'Hmmm . . .' The professor was an innocent chap. He was hardly 4 years older to us. He was one of the engineers who graduated from our college and opted to stay back and take up a career in teaching. 'So what do you suggest? Shall we inform the college about it?' He asked us.

'No sir. Just report to the College that the IV was successful and everything went on well.' I replied.

'But that will be unethical.'

'From one angle, it is a lie and is unethical sir. But look at it from this angle sir, if the college finds out that the class went all the way to Bangalore and came back without attending IV, they will question you first. You will be screwed for wasting one working day, for hiring a bus and fuelling and most importantly, for your poor co-ordination.' He thought deeply for a moment. 'Unnecessarily, you will be suspended. You need the pay, especially since you are getting married next month.'

'You already asked me to not inform the management about guys boozing inside the bus.' He said with disappointment. 'Guess this trip was planned to be a flop.' He moved towards the bus and boarded it.

'I thought he will blast you for conducting this, in his language, "flop industrial visit".' Chris whispered.

'He is a nice guy.' I replied. 'Guess we should buy him a beer.'

Chacko and the rest of the guys laughed uncontrollably as we boarded the bus again. Prasad went to the bus driver and shouted 'I am out of beer. Stop by the shop on your right in JP Nagar. It is exactly 2 kms from this location. Take the short route. I will help you.'

'You know the roads in Bangalore?' Samuel asked him, surprised with Prasad's knowledge about the city.

'No. I know where they sell beer and whisky.'

'In Bangalore?'

'In all the cities in India. It is important for boozers like us.'

'Do you know I took your database management paper in the 3rd semester and you scored 0 in it?' Samuel asked.

'You are a professor?' Prasad asked, looking greatly amused.

I silently grinned at Samuel, who shook his head in disappointment.

'Learning the wrong things is in his blood.' Param informed Samuel.

'And what about you?'

'I am his roommate for God's sake. I learn from him.'

* * *

'Wow. I just realized that the guys in our class actually liked travelling all the way and come back from Bangalore in a remodeled 1970 bus, which could hardly touch 60kms per hour.'

'What did Newton do when an apple fell on his head?'

'He discovered gravity.'

'Exactly. These guys have understood the fun of travelling in this trip. Most of them eat and pee in the same place.'

'How is that related to gravity?'

'Gravity = fun. You don't get it?'

'Dude.' Chris thought for a moment and said nothing.

The trip was fun and everyone thoroughly enjoyed it, except Jeffrey and his gang. As we were busy discussing about all the fun we had in class, the director came walking into our class room.

'The ass is lucky.' I knew he was referring to me and I immediately got up from my place. Other than the Facebook incident I was caught by the director in another incident too, for participating with a girl in LSN College (Shruthi and Preethi) which was against the college rules.

'He gets a week off.'

'Why sir?' I asked politely.

'Creating fake letters are you?' he roared and gave me a tight slap. I said nothing and lowered my head. *Jeffrey had actually informed about me!* Now, I understood who he was. A third rated cheap insecure bastard! Thank God, I was not like him. Everyone sat silently and no one supported, as everyone (including Param and Prasad) knew that if they raise their voice, it will end up they also getting suspended from College.

'Sorry sir.'

'Sorry, my foot. Thank God that it is just a week. Any other day it would have been semester drop.'

*   *   *

February 2008:

'I will feel bad for you.' Chitra stated sadly.

'I too feel bad for me.' I replied. 'I am sure Chris would have missed me in College.'

'Totally' Chris accepted. 'Being with Deepakh for a week was like being in hell.'

'I know why you say that!' Chitra smiled. ''Cause he keeps asking about me to you.'

'How did you know?' Chris grew suspicious.

'Dumbo' Chitra replied 'You have told me that a thousand times.' Chris personally requested me not to invite Deepakh to any restaurant where he brought Chitra along.

I saw two hot chicks in white t-shirt and blue jeans take seats next to our table. They were clearly from the northern region of India and I was sure they were Punjabis, as their cheek were pink in color and they looked good.

'Pay the bill today!' I whispered to Chris. 'Give me the cash. I will act as if I am paying for the bill in front of the babes.'

'I knew you will come down to that. That's why I came here with empty pockets.' Chris whispered back.

'Seeing somewhere?' Chitra asked Chris quickly, as she noticed Chris and me distracted since the arrival of the chicks.

'Yes . . .' Chris blabbered. 'Eh . . . no sorry'

'Don't lose yourself to someone else.' Chitra warned Chris.

'I am ready to lose to a beautiful girl like you.'

'Fool.' Chitra growled. 'I don't get flattered.'

'Ok.' Chris felt insulted. 'But 99 out of 100 girls would have smiled for that.'

'I am not one of them.'

I did not give a damn about their discussion and kept staring at the new arrivals, only to be halted after one of them pointed to their slippers.

'They noticed you noticing them.' Chris informed.

'I knew that. Wanted to know what they would do?' I covered up. 'And honestly, as I told to you before, it is tough to find girls of my type.'

'Guys, foods ready.' Chitra ordered the server to serve the food. Chitra spotted a puppy and exclaimed 'Chris we must have a cat. Look at it, it is so cute.'

'It is a dog!' Chris corrected her.

'I know. But it looks like a cat. Small, fluffy and sweet. Will you buy and give me one?'

'Cat or dog?'

'A cat'

'Sure.' Chris assured.

'When?'

'Sure means I will look into it.'

'But I want it now. NOW! You are not even taking any steps for marrying me.'

'I will buy you one by this weekend.'

'Give it in writing.'

'You must bring your wallet the next time you come out.' I whispered to Chris.

'Why?'

'Girls will not like you.'

'Chitra likes me, not you.' Chris replied.

'Hmmm . . .'

Chapter 15

Realization

'I replied a Yes at least ten times to your message and you kept asking me!' Chitra said.

'I know. But I wanted to be sure that you did not change your mind about coming here. Seeing you here has cleared my doubt.' Chris replied.

'My God. You are mad!'

'Yeah. A good mad guy.'

'Whatever!' Chitra said, as she registered for the events in SVIT College, Bangalore. Knowing the fact that if we participated in any event with a girl in Chennai, we would be noticed by the college authorities, we decided to travel to Bangalore and participate there, not because I was desperate to participate, but because Chitra was desperate to participate with Chris. And to Chris' dismay, Deepakh accompanied us!

'And there was a time when Deepakh never came out with us.' I remembered.

'Past is past.' Deepakh answered.

'So how did you get her number?' Chris asked Deepakh.

'She gave it to me.' Deepakh said.

'I think she gave you the wrong number.'

'No! She gave me the right number.' Deepakh got it from me!

'So this is where the hunks hide?' Chitra asked Chris. 'Look at the amount they spend to look good.'

Chris said nothing as I got our ID cards and joined the gang. 'Lucky that I am suspended because of which I can travel wherever and whenever I want.' I smiled. 'I am under suspension for helping everyone come to Bangalore and it has helped me come to Bangalore!'

'Yes' Deepakh moved closer to Chitra, only to be stopped by Chris. 'If not for you, I would have not got an opportunity to spend a whole day in fairy land with the damsel herself.'

'This is Bangalore, not fairy land!' Chris shouted.

'Wherever Chitra goes, its fairy land!'

'Right' Chris knew Deepakh went out of hand over the past few months and was actually not bothered of what he said. 'You know what' he turned to me and started 'Here is some interesting fact that might cheer you up.'

'Go on'

'Poor Raman has participated in 50 mock interview events in cultural programs and has not won in any!'

'Out in 50 innings for a duck!'

'Exactly' Chris smiled.

'He was licking the wrong asses and it did not work out for him.' I chuckled. 'They helped him get entry passes but not winning passes!'

'We don't have to worry about that.' Chitra smiled. 'Our smile is our certificate.'

'I have experienced that in my life.' I thought about Shruthi and Preethi. 'I will have to accept that, without doubt!'

'Tools of destruction!' Chris said. 'Cost me 10K already.'

'Keep smiling' Deepakh kept staring at her.

'No worries. I will cost you a lot more!' She chuckled and hugged Chris. 'My mother has told me that if you help others you will receive the favor ten times more.'

'Beggars are not stock brokers to help you get back your investment. It is a one side process. Money lost is lost.' Chris cried.

'Justin!' Deepakh caught my shirt and shouted 'You will be shocked to see this'

'Hi fucker'

'I know that voice.' I turned back and saw Jeffrey standing. How the hell did he get here? I looked around and saw none of the *terror gang* guys out there, but was shocked to see someone I had not expected to meet out there. 'Shruthi and Preethi?'

'How do you do?' Shruthi spoke. 'And I am seriously sorry because I forgot your name. What do they call you?'

'Justin' I was not impressed. *I hate girls with attitude!*

'Ah! Justin the joker.' She smiled unwillingly. 'I found one idiot to accompany us. And I know he is not totally unknown to you.'

'He is my fucked up class mate.' I turned to Jeffrey. 'Your committee makes rules and you break it?'

'Looks like the suspension period is being utilized properly by my dearest foe'

'Fuck off. You are lucky to be in shape now. It won't take me more than a few seconds to break you to bits and pieces.'

'Let's see about that.'

'Shut up the two of you' Deepakh roared and interrupted us. 'Jeffrey, get going. Prove your mettle on stage, not here.'

'If not for Deepakh, you would have become chutney for my evening dosa.' Jeffrey informed me.

'Ha ha! The donkey brays.' I roared as Jeffrey walked off with Shruthi and Preethi to the room where Dumb-Charades was organized. 'Now I hate that guy more than how much he hates me. He will surely get it from me.'

'I understand your feelings.' Chris stated sadly.

'I hope you understand my feeling too.' Deepakh said.

'Yours is called jealousy. Not feelings.'

'Jealousy is a kind of feeling.' Deepakh said. 'Hatred in its amateur state!' I grinned.

'And considering the fact that you are going to be our Dumb-Charades partner is already giving me Goosebumps.' Chris said.

'Me?' Deepakh asked me quickly.

'Never mind. And worse is, Chitra being our Ad-Zap partner.' Chris said disappointedly.

'I don't understand why you are scared about Chitra being our partner in the competition.'

'Chitra might actually take center stage and make me promise in front of everyone that I will serve food to beggars.'

'And why would you do that?'

'I will do anything that Chitra will tell me to.'

'Someone mentioned my name?' Chitra asked. 'And who were they? Baby, don't tell me you know them?'

'I don't know them. They are strangers.'

'And what were you talking with those STRANGERS?'

'Nothing. They were asking directions to the auditorium.' Deepakh chuckled as Chris blabbered.

'I believe you.' Chitra assured. 'I seriously do.'

'Don't do that.' Deepakh made use of this opportunity. 'He is a very good friend of those girls. He even participated with them in LSN College!'

'Did you do that?' Chitra asked with anger and Deepakh slowly grinned. 'Did you?'

'It was Justin's idea to take them in our team for Ad-Zap.' Chris defended.

'Oh' Suddenly Chitra smiled. 'You must have called them to join our team today. It would have completed our team for Ad-Zap.' She said as Chris smiled brightly. 'You missed it, baby!' And walked off smiling

Chris caught an astonished Deepakh and said 'She is not my bed mate to fall for such stupid reasons. 5 years relationship man, 5 years!'

'I see that!' Deepakh said as we followed Chitra.

'Hey!' Jeffrey came running out of the room as Shruthi came running behind him. 'Where the fuck are you going?' I asked him.

'Not today. Go back to your house, Justin.' He said running out of the college. He turned to look at me and screamed 'Run, I am warning you.'

'Is something wrong inside?' I asked Chris as Jeffrey ran out like a mad man.

'I think I know' I said, as I found our first year friend Divya come out of the class room.

'Awesome!' Chris said. 'What the hell is she doing here? No wonder Jeffrey ran.'

Jeffrey did not even wait for the local bus, as he got into a moving auto and absconded.

'I know you!' Divya said as she came running towards me. 'You were one of the bastards in that fucked up class, weren't you?'

'Yes' I smiled.

'Remember the sandwich you gave me?'

'He he'

'You still share spoilt sandwiches with your friends, fucker? And you only share spoilt sandwiches or anything else also? Huh?'

'You think we should follow Jeffrey?' I got no reply and turned to see no one standing next to me.

'He left a few seconds ago.' She said.

'Oh my God!' I shouted as I ran out of the College, to find Chris boarding an auto which I chased down and got into.

'What about Chitra?'

'They will be fine without us.'

'How do you say that?'

'They are history now. Like my love, studies, money and family will soon be history.' Chris cried.

'And the present?'

'Police case, chappals, women burning our pictures.'

'No wonder Jeffrey ran.'

'Yeah'

'Man I am still a virgin.' I cried to him. 'And I doubted Jeffrey.'

Ah ah . . . stop it stop it. We heard a woman moaning in the auto.

'Is there a video player in this auto that is playing a porn flick?' I asked the auto guy.

'It's my mobile. I like this tone.' Chris smiled. 'Got it a few days back'

'Sick.'

'Hey baby.' He said as he picked up the phone. 'No baby; my mother is not feeling well and I had to leave in a hurry. Sorry babe I could not inform you.' His smile faded slowly. 'I am serious baby. No, I won't do that.' He was not smiling anymore. 'Ok, I will be back in a minute. I guarantee you that.' He switched off the mobile 'Take us back to the college.' He ordered the auto driver.

'What happened?'

'She won't let me leave.' Chris cried. 'Wait a minute. We left Deepakh back there with Chitra. Oh my God! We must go back.' He roared.

'What?'

'The polls say that.'

'Who voted in the polls?'

'I.'

'Ok. We see Divya, act as if have short term memory loss and say we don't know her and get out of the scene.'

'That worked in a Hollywood flick. And the actor had tattoos all over his body and a camera.'

'I have a camera mobile. Almost qualified'

'Baby, you are back.' Chitra and Deepakh were waiting for us outside, as we got down from the auto.

'Yes, always available for you.'

'Ran away didn't you?'

'Yes' Deepakh answered 'Why did you guys come back? It was going well out here.'

'No Chitra, no.' Chris said, as he moved closer to her to convince. 'We went to a place where they are serving homemade curd rice and tomato rice. The ambience and the food quality are good. Maybe we can go there for lunch.' He smiled. 'And above all we left Deepakh behind too. I will never ditch you in a city like Bangalore with Deepakh.'

'Oh . . . how thoughtful of you, my love.' She said. 'But anyways, even if you would have found my way back as this is my hometown. And so is yours!'

'I forgot'

'I will take that as always, for the plate of curd rice you promised to buy me.' Chitra said quickly. She was like a chameleon that changed colors quickly. 'More than one plate is preferred.'

'Ok.'

'And my friend wanted to meet you two. She said she knew two assholes with the same names. I wanted to show to her you two are not them.'

'Yes, until or unless it is Divya, we are not assholes.' Chris whispered.

'Meet Divya.' Chitra smiled.

Divya came walking from behind and laughed loudly. 'Dating an asshole? My God Chitra, I thought you were better than that.'

'How do you know her? She was not even our school mate.'

'But she was dating our school mate.'

'Oh' Chris said.

'You don't think we called you and disturbed you at night right?' I asked Divya.

'No. Not at all. Jeffrey ran the minute he saw me. Maybe he was scared that I will ask him about that.'

'So did you find the guy?'

'Actually the truth is I did not receive any calls. No one disturbed me.'

'Then why did you leave college?'

'For a guy in this college!' She chuckled.

'So there was a guy. I was right.' Chris' face glittered.

'A perfect plan. And the asses in our class were fighting each other for this chick. Funny world we live in.'

*   *   *

'If our bus would have been scheduled for tomorrow, we could have met my parents.' Chris said. 'I don't think we will have the time.'

'Some other time. Not an issue.' I smiled.

Time ticked slowly and I sat with a speechless with Chris, till 12:00 PM, before we met my school mate Sonu who had participated in paper presentation. He was brimming with confidence and I was happy for him.

He had joined IIT Madras and was a regular in all the cultural events.

Outside, Chitra was chatting with Divya.

'You will win dude, for sure.' I informed Sonu. He was a nerd and had participated in over 22 paper presentations and not lost in any. The last time I met him was in School during the final exams.

'There is this guy called Suresh who told us he does not lose in any paper presentations. I'm sure he would have won 50 prizes by now. Do you know him by any chance?' Chris asked.

'I know him very well. We take turns in participating in different colleges. Where he fixes I don't go and where is am assured of a win, he boycotts.'

'Oh, so you guys take turns in winning. What about the rest who come here hoping to win?'

'Their problem.' Balaji said. 'They can win the second place though.'

'He said the same thing.' I said.

'We are allies.'

'Yeah, second is something to fight for.' I thought. 'So what are you intending to do with so many winning certificates?'

'I never thought about that.' Balaji said. 'All that I keep thinking about is winning'

*　　*　　*

It was 2:00 PM and got on stage to participate in the event "block 'n' tackle". The topic given was *movies*. I started talking with confidence and people represent in the hall applauded me. The judge was an English staff member working in that college, who pretended as if he knew everything. He decided to screw my luck by buzzing a bell as a sign for me to switch from defending the topic to attacking the topic.

"Tring, tring, tring, tring" He kept buzzing like a mad man. I lost count of the number of times the bell sounded. I spoke continuously and at one point I started talking against the topic when I was supposed to talk for the topic. *How can a guy speak with the bell ringing the whole time? He is supposed to say the words 'block' or 'tackle' and not buzz a bloody bell.*

Three minutes were up and my performance, which started with a bang, ended ordinarily.

'I am next.' Deepakh smiled. 'You spoke well on stage. Good to see you can actually talk.'

'I think you will win.' Chris told me.

'I don't know.' I said.

'I meant the second place. Deepakh will obviously win it!' He smiled.

'When is your turn?' I asked Chris cheekily.

'Not today. I am sticking with ad-zap.'

'Scared?'

Chris smiled. 'Kind of yes'

'What happened to Dumb Charades?' Chitra asked.

'Deepakh moved like a snake to enact the word *body.*' I said. 'And I thought it was anaconda.'

'Sad he is not good in acting.' Chris said.

Deepakh spoke with confidence and his English was far superior to mine. The audience gave a standing ovation to him and I was happy to lose to a guy of his talent.

'We have our last participant for the day . . .' The host announced.

'Only Deepakh and you spoke well. If this person screws, you are winning for sure.' Chris assured me.

'Hanna from Women's Christian College, Chennai.'

'The name sounds familiar.' I said.

'Look at her. She looks familiar too.' Chris pointed to the girl that I saw days back in MIT, Chennai. 'You can forget the 2nd prize too!'

'Oh shit! It is the same Hanna.' I said with a big wide open mouth, as she stepped into the stage and started talking, in the same style as she always does, "like a non-stop train".

'I remember her informing us that wherever there is Block 'n' Tackle and Jam, she will be there.'

'I remember her saying JAM and debate.' I remembered. 'Not block 'n' tackle.'

'Something' Chris said. 'Just check with the judge whether the person bagging the third price gets something. I don't think you will be a winner or a runner-up with Deepakh and Hanna around.'

'You are right.' Hanna spoke as well as Deepakh, but the only difference being she had more valid points in her defense and offense on the topic. She spoke with confidence and modulated as well as any politician would and the whole audience applauded her. It came to me as a surprise to see that none of the other participants were even confident to talk for the complete time allotted.

'Tell me man.' I whispered in Chris' ears. 'Do I stand a chance to get into the top 2? As in, do I have an outside chance?'

'If I was the judge for this competition, I don't think that will happen.'

'And why do you say that?'

'You had no valid points, neither in your defense nor in your offense.'

The results came out at 3:00PM and I bagged the 3rd price, losing to none other than Hanna, who bagged the 1st price and Deepakh the 2nd.

'Ladies first' I told Chris and walked across to the judge. 'Do I get anything?'

'A certificate'

'Money?'

'Sorry'

'I defeated you.' Hanna smiled at Deepakh. She seriously seemed to like him. 'And you spoke well too.' She turned to me 'Never knew the stone spoke!'

'I'm happy to lose to you.' I spoke the truth.

'Will beat you next time' Deepakh added

'Ah ha!' She laughed out loud. 'Nice.' She walked off.

'Happy to lose to you!' Chris repeated. 'Never knew you loved to lose! Not after losing for over a year'

'I love losing to good looking girls. And I at least got a certificate'

'Good looking girls or "girl"?'

*　　*　　*

'Whether we win or not, I don't want that bastard Jeffrey to win in Ad-Zap.'

'Good news for you.'

'What is it?'

'Shruthi and Preethi did not win in Dumb-Charades.' Chris roared.

'What?'

'Yes. Everyone replicated their tactic here. And understandably the judge was replaced by a girl at the last moment as everyone ended up getting words like money, hair, nose, ears and other simple words.'

'Ad-zap now!' Chitra interfered. 'Let's go.'

Shruthi and Preethi formed a team with Jeffrey and another guy who I had never met before.

'What do you think Shruthi and Preethi will do this time around?' Chris asked me.

'As usual, walk and win.'

'We have Hanna in our team.' Chris reminded me. 'That's something that will work out for us.'

'Let's see . . . I'm not pinning my hopes on her.'

Preethi's team went up on stage and Shruthi and Preethi started walking around the stage. Jeffrey was not seen on stage and I was sure he was standing back stage, petrified!

Nevertheless, the crowds went crazy and cheered for the team.

'Next on stage Chitra's team.' Divya, the host for the event informed. The judge was a bald headed man in his early thirties. They introduced him as a theater artist. 'Team, your product is IPod.'

'Sing a song.' Chitra ordered us.

'What?'

'Some shitty song'

'Do as she says.' Chris told me. 'Some shitty song'

Chitra stood in the center of the stage and we stood by her side and started singing "summer of 69". The audience rolled on the floor with laughter.

'I feel insulted.' I took a second to take a quick breath and continued singing. 'And I forgot the lyrics too.'

Chitra started dancing on stage. 'Bloody shit. She is a professional dancer.' Chris roared.

The whole crowd went mad, except Shruthi and Preethi.

'Why didn't you tell me that she dances?' I asked Chris. We stopped singing as the whole crowd started dancing along with Chitra.

'Dude, I came to know that she dances only a second ago. Never knew the savior of beggars even dances.'

Our time was up, to the crowd's disappointment.

Shruthi came up to us and said 'We need to learn a lot from you.' While Chitra was still beaming. 'I don't have any dancing skills.'

'I'm ready to teach.' Chitra said happily.

'Thanks a lot!'

'You don't have to do that.' Chris interrupted. 'They have other tactics to win the competitions.' Chris laughed. 'Today talent won over catwalk.'

'Excuse me?'

'Losers!'

'Oh!' Shruthi did not reply as a disappointed Rejo and Preethi pulled her out and left.

'Your dance steps were just too good.'

'Thanks baby.'

We waited down as another team took center stage. They were from Manipal University and they brought the stage to life. Dance, emotions, acting, jingle, they did everything at one go on stage.

'Awesome!' I said to myself.

To my surprise, everyone who came on stage after that kept doing the same. Everyone was skilled and I seriously felt that the person who would bag the 1st place there would surely be a team that is worth.

'Dude, this place is too good.' I whispered to Deepakh. 'I will be proud to go back home as a loser, today. Not because I am happy we will lose, but because we will go back home as proud losers to a really good team.'

'I will have to agree to that.'

We did lose, but I was happy about that. I had learnt won thing clear and sound today; talent will be rewarded, maybe if not initially but surely as time goes by.

'You think I will win the something in block 'n' tackle when Hanna and Deepakh are around?' I asked Chris.

'I don't think so!'

'Why do you say that?'

'You said it man, ladies first!'

*   *   *

We had a sumptuous meal and stepped out of the restaurant, situated inside the bus stop in Majestic. It was 9 in the evening and our bus was scheduled for 9:30 from Majestic, Bangalore.

'May I have your number?' I asked Hanna. Dinner was good, but it cost 1800 bucks and Chris and Chitra were busy discussing about that. We had invited Hanna to join us in our journey back home, as she was travelling back home alone. Thanks to Deepakh, she accepted the proposal and joined us.

'I don't give my number to guys. I don't like their mobiles having my name in it.'

'Let me be the first then.'

'Ok, what have you done to earn my number?' She asked me. 'And you will not be the first for sure' She turned to Deepakh and smiled

I thought for a moment. *It is a mobile number for God's sake. What should I do to earn it? Can't I just have it?*

'But what are you going to do with it? Disturb me with forwards?'

'No. Just ask some questions.'

'What questions?'

'About the cultural programs you will be attending and the dates for the same.'

'Can't you find it on your own?'

'I can. But why waste my time browsing and searching for it when I have a reliable source.'

'Excuse me! Even I browse the internet to know these details. I don't own a magic calendar that shows when and where I have to go.'

'Just give me your number. Questions need not be restricted to events alone!'

'Man, you sound desperate. I wouldn't dare give it to you. That might be the biggest mistake in my life.'

'You don't want me to beg.' I was desperate.

She smiled. 'Never knew my mobile number cost so much that you are begging for it.'

'It is worth thousands for me.' I quickly took out my mobile and created a contact in her name. 'Now your number please!'

She smiled and gave it to me.

'I will give you a missed call.'

'Not needed.' She replied. 'I don't want your number. And remember, don't dare call me.' Hanna warned.

'Why?' I asked Hanna quickly.

'I won't answer calls from anonymous people.'

'God will not forgive us for spending 1800 bucks for a single meal. There are so many people out there who are not able to afford curd rice and dosa for a single meal.' Chitra cried.

'Chitra, there are people who spend 1800 bucks for a single dish!'

'I won't do that.' Deepakh interrupted.

'Why do you always poke your nose in other's business?' Chris asked Deepakh.

'Cause that is my business!'

'I am not bothered about others. We must not come here again. We could have rather given the money to hungry beggars outside the temple near my house.'

'Can't I rather spend it here and eat good food?'

'No.' Chitra said and joined Hanna and me. 'What's happening?'

'Introvert!' I smiled.

'So she did not give you her number?' Deepakh asked me, as Chitra took Hanna with her and boarded the bus.

'She gave me a number.'

'That's cool.'

'Why do you say that?'

'She gave me a number that is now out of order.'

'That sounds dumb. That means she is trying to ignore you.' Deepakh consoled me.

'No. It means she wants me to prove how much I am desperate for her. This practically means she wants me to earn it.'

'So that's means Chitra wants me to earn it.' Deepakh added quickly. 'No wonder she is also avoiding me.'

*　　*　　*

'So it's just the three of us!' I sat at the seats in the bus next to Hanna and Chitra. 'Isn't it nice?' Chris and Deepakh were fast asleep.

'I see over 50 people in this bus. Better check your eyes.'

'Others matter little, especially when there is this special someone next to you.'

'Special someone?' Hanna was not impressed 'You are not special!'

'I am.' I smiled. 'Everyone is special in some way.'

'And how are you special?'

'Hmmm . . . You and I are like Will turner and Jack sparrow.'

'I don't think they liked each other.' Hanna reminded me.

'But they worked together.'

'Not convincing.'

'Ok . . . Like Samwise and Frodo.'

'I am not in a mission and you will never be prepared to sacrifice your life for me.'

'Try me.' I said. 'By the way you carry the burden of never losing the 1st place to anyone, including Deepakh, in Block 'n' Tackle.'

She laughed. 'You guys have competed against me just twice in your life time. That is not a burden to me.' She said. 'And this might be the last!' She chuckled.

'May be we can take this a step forward . . .' I said. 'Like Aragorn and Arwen.'

'What?' She shouted. 'I won't sacrifice my immortality for you!'

'I thought lover's do anything for their loved ones.' I said.

'They do.' Hanna said. 'Sadly I am not your lover and will never be.'

'Never say never again.' I said quickly. 'Anything might happen tomorrow.'

'You don't love me, do you?'

I thought for a moment. 'Do you?'

'No no.'

'I like you, but don't know whether it is called love.'

'It better not be love.' Hanna said 'I don't want love.' She was getting restless.

'You won't have many friends if you don't appreciate love. And considering the fact that you don't have an Orkut or a Facebook account comes to say you are not interested in having friends. You should seriously reconsider your ideologies and start living a new life.'

'I do not prefer social life. It sucks.'

'Facebook sucks mainly because it is now more like a dating network.'

'Let people live the way they want to.' Hanna replied.

'Then you must let me live the way I want to.'

'I am not interfering.' Hanna replied. 'Go to sleep. Any other day, if you would have said what you told to me to any girl, you would have been dead by now.'

'I did not say anything wrong.'

'I did not like it.' She closed her eyes and concluded. 'I am happy with the people who are around. No point in having friends who will only contribute to my phone bills.'

'I'm glad that you are happy to have me around.' I said happily. 'I am special. I told you.'

Hanna said nothing.

* * *

"I can finally see your house today." I thought
happily. I always imagined her to be a princess living
in a house that'd have a beautiful garden filled with
fragrant flowers Hanna liked. She would take a stroll in
the evening, brushing her cheeks against the flowers and
kissing them softly.

'So when do we meet next?' I asked her. We reached
Adyar, where all of us got down.

'I don't think that will happen.'

'Why do you keep saying that?' Deepakh and the rest
were half asleep.

'I am leaving to a foreign nation next month.' She
smiled. 'And with me not in Orkut or Facebook, it's bye.'
She smiled. 'And the number I gave to you is my number,
which got disconnected last week.' She smiled. 'Bye to
you, to cultural competitions and to India.'

I said nothing and stood numb.

'Bye.' Deepakh said.

'Bye' I added.

'Bye.' She smiled, finally to me and caught an auto
and left.

'She left eh?' Chris asked me, wiping his eyes and
face with some water.

'She is leaving to a foreign nation next month.' I said
sadly.

*   *   *

'You know sometimes I think she is not even from this
planet.'

'You mean to say that she is an alien'

'Yeah, that's what I meant.'

'Oh. Then she may be she is from Venus.' Chris said.
'I read a book which said that the girls are not from this
planet. WOMEN ARE FROM VENUS.'

'The title in full has MEN ARE FROM MARS! It does not mean "they are from there"! It was just a catchy line that sounded good.'

'Oh! And I always thought they were from Venus.' Chris was disappointed. 'You know I was thinking about writing a book on my own.'

'Wow! And what do you call it?'

'*A Man has an anus, and his friend uses his penis!*' Chris said. 'Sounds catchy?'

'Hmmm . . .' It was disgusting. 'I might not grab your books first copy. That is totally gay!'

'Yeah! And the lead in the book is called Rejo.'

'I think you are misusing his name.'

'Not until he complains.' Chris put up his evil smile in his face. 'So Chris, you told me that your conscience told you that you will surely get Hanna?'

'Yeah right!' I said. 'And my conscience told me I think I will get her because I think I will get her!'

'Because your conscience thinks what you want to think.'

'Funny, that's what my conscience also told me.'

'Leave who told you what, but I do appreciate the confidence you have in yourself.'

'I believe in a win-win situation.'

'Hmmm . . . What does she win if she gets you?'

'Obviously first things first, long nights!'

'And anything else?'

'Hmmm . . . I need to think about that.' I thought for a moment. 'But your girlfriend Chitra, she's different. She has something called a 'helping nature' inculcated in her.'

'That's because Chitra was born in a family that runs an NGO for poor kids and beggars.'

'You never told me that.'

'I did now.'

'Oh . . .' I said. 'So this means her family is also like her?'

'Possible' Chris said.

'Excuse me.' Deepakh stated quickly. 'Can we get back to business?'

'Business? You must be aware of the fact that we are from the working class. And between, Hanna did talk well with you. She must have surely given you her number.'

'No. I did not want it, as I needed only Chitra's.'

'Dude' Chris said. 'The whole world knows that you are joking when you say you like Chitra. You talk about her only when I am around.' Chris kept his hand over Deepakh. 'I have had enough of your lousy jokes. If you ever loved a girl, I assume it would have been Hanna, at least from the girls I know.'

Deepakh did not reply.

'Ok. So what do you want to do?'

'Good question.' Deepakh replied. 'Since you brought me here, so you can answer that!'

'Hmmm . . . A cup of coffee in a petty shop?'

'We came all the way from Chennai to Chengalpattu Medical College for that?'

'Hmmm . . . I am not sick and so I don't have to get admitted in the hospital here.'

'You must thank Deepakh for this disaster. He told us they have ad-zap, block 'n' tackle and some other events here.'

'Thank you'

'I see a list with the name of all the events.' I said. 'And I see that there a lot of people who have travelled all the way from Chennai and other parts of India to come and participate in the events here.'

'These names look Greek and Latin to me.' Chris looked into the list. 'They've given Tamil names to all the events. Man, what crap!'

'Hey, we can participate in this event *Katri paper.*' Deepakh announced.

'What the fuck is that?'

'They call it Collage in English.' He said. 'They have "block 'n' tackle" and Ad-Zap also.'

'That's cool.' I was happy to hear that. 'So we can register for that.'

'But, we should talk in Tamil.'

'Fuck. Ok, explain collage.'

'Cut, paste, write, draw and paint.' Deepakh said.

'That's it?' I said.

'I think so.'

'Wow! That sounds rather easy.' I was confident until I saw a group of guys carrying bags into the drawing hall where the stage for collage was set up. 'Hmmm! Looks like the participants have packed a lot of food from home.' I laughed.

'They are carrying bags with a lot of materials they can make use of in the competition.'

'Oh cool! And where are our materials?'

Rejo took out a newspaper and showed it to us.

'That's the daily paper.'

'Today's paper.' He smiled. 'I brought this for the competition.'

'You mean to say this is all that we have?' I was hoping he was joking.

'Yes.'

My head was spinning. 'Oh ok.' *Asshole*

'May I read it?' Chris asked.

'Sure.' Deepakh smiled. 'It has an article about the actress who slept with a Swami.'

'Whoa!' Chris was excited. 'I am following that story closely.'

We entered the room. All opened their bags and took their items out. We could see some of the items they carried along with them for this competition. 'Scissors, glue, Paper, charts, magazines, stickers, pens, pencils, sketchers, paint brush, crayons, and magic pens.' Chris was also looking at everyone around us. 'And we have brought along today's newspaper! Bloody hell'

'I brought along. Not WE.' Deepakh took pride for the newspaper he brought with him. 'I will take credit for that!'

'I carry the newspaper to my toilet every morning you asshole!' I roared. 'You could have asked us to bring something along with us, if you found it a burden to do it yourself.'

'You wouldn't have come here if I'd told you that collage is the only event we are eligible to participate in this college.'

'He has a point' Chris interrupted 'and you know the article says that the actress confessed that she was learning to recite prayers at midnight in the Swami's room. Hmmm! Wonder what prayers the Swami was teaching her at midnight!' He smirked.

'They are giving a chart to every team for cutting and paste.' Deepakh said. 'Whoa! Now that's cool'

'But what how will you paste when you don't have glue with you.'

'Age old technique. We will we use spit to stick things.' He said.

Disgusting

I said nothing and went directly to the host who was handing over the materials. 'Hi.'

'Hi.' The host smiled. 'Here's your chart.'

'Thanks' I went closer to her and waited for the other participants to leave. 'Your college looks awesome.'

'Thanks' She was flattered.

'I am serious and having girls like you adds to the beauty of this college.'

She smiled. 'Looks like you are trying to get something from me.'

'No. I am just an admirer of beauty.' She was smiling. She was tall and had pride written all over her fair skin.

She looked like a Brahmin from down south of Tamil Nadu. 'And if I do not admire you, it means I do not have taste.'

'Sweet of you'

'I can go on.' Honestly, I was in no mood to do that.

'What do you want?'

'A few magazines, glue stick and a scissor.'

She handed it over to me. 'All the best and hope you win.'

'Your wishes will suffice this humble soul.' *What a cheap thing to say. All for some stationery.*

I went back to the table where Chris and Deepakh were waiting for me. They stared at me.

'Don't look at me like that' I said proudly. 'It is called charisma.'

'Fucker . . . she is coming over to each and every participant and giving scissors, glue, and magazines.'

I turned back and saw her do the same. 'Oh!'

'You went and saved her the time to carry the things up to our table.' Chris said. 'You did her a favor.'

'Bloody I wasted time in flattering her. And I don't think she would have bought it.'

'If we lose'

'You told me we are in India.'

'Don't I have the right to crack a joke?'

'It cost me dignity.'

The timer was set and we started working with our materials. The topic given was "INDIA BURNING."

'I have an idea.' Deepakh started.

'I sure hope it is good.' Chris replied.

'Why not cut some pictures of the present ministers of our country and paste it?'

'That's too straight forward.' I said. 'The host won't buy that! India burning should be something related with the after affects.'

'Then you must show dry taps and middle class men and women travelling in crowded buses with empty pockets.' He said.

'Yes! That's right. By the way, from where is that smoke coming from?' We looked around and saw holding a half burnet chart in his hands.

'If the chart is burnt, does that mean we get disqualified from the competition?' Chris asked.

'Without a chart there is no competition for us.' I said 'What the fuck did you do?'

'Tested the lighter I found outside the hall. It is working.' Chris smiled.

'Bugger that cost us half of our chart.'

'Look at the positive part. We still have a half with us.' Chris said. 'And I did not do it on purpose.'

'The topic is India burning and half of our chart is burnt!' Deepakh cried.

How cruel can life be!

'You think the judge will buy it if we tell her that we burnt the chart for the event?'

'You know I remember a sentence from the book.'

'What?'

'I will buy that!' Chris said. 'And that sounds creative.'

*   *   *

'What is this?' The judge came up to our desk and saw our half burnt chart, with pictures of people crying at the top half of the chart and politicians laughing at the bottom half of the chart.

'Indian Burning.' I said. 'I burnt the chart to show that because of the work of many corrupt people in our country, it is suffering.'

'It is going to the dogs.' Deepakh added as the judge's eyes twinkled.

'Oh!'

'The chart shows that the fire is moving fast and quick.' I turned the chart and showed pictures of people standing in a line. 'The only solution we have at hand is to join hands and work against corruption and stop the country from going to the dogs.'

The judge said nothing for a second as two volunteers, who followed her to the table, where we stood and displayed our chart, whispered into her ears about our performance. 'Nice!' the judge finally spoke 'Something new and creative. And I thought your chart got burnt because of some freak accident.'

'No no.' I smiled. 'We would never do that. Everything has a purpose.'

'Good.' She wrote something in the score sheet she carried and said 'All the best.' And she walked off with the volunteers to the next table.

'She actually bought that!' Chris said with surprise. 'But honestly speaking I had a major part to play in this event.' Chris said. 'If not for me, we would have not submitted an awesome collage.'

'I agree with you.' Deepakh said happily.

The results came and we bagged the second prize.

'That's a surprise.' I said. 'I wonder who won the first prize.'

'That will be us.' A guy came and shook hands with me. 'Stephen from Madras Medical College.'

'Congrats. I'm Justin.' I smiled.

'Quite creative, your work.' He said, as he observed our chart closely.

'May I take a look at your chart?'

'Yes.' He smiled and showed it to us. 'My God!' Chris, Deepakh and I roared as we saw the chart with blood scattered over the chart. 'That is blood?'

'Yes.'

'And you cut your hand for this event?' His hand was bandaged.

'No.' He came close to me. 'I broke my hand in a bike accident in the streets of Chennai some days ago.'

'Oh! That's common in Chennai.'

'Yes.' He said. 'We used a cup of chicken blood bought from the butcher shop nearby. We are generally well prepared. My hand is bandaged almost the entire year around, but considering the fact that the judge is a girl, I let them think that I cut my hand for the event.'

'Interesting' I replied. 'Doctors are doctors.'

What a freak!

'And I thought we were smart.' Chris said quickly to me.

Stephen smiled and packed up his materials.

'I am actually happy to lose to you.' I informed him.

Chapter 16

The big news

<u>*January 2009:*</u>

'Dude, 12 months, two semesters, 35 different competitions and' I was devastated. Thankfully from the 6th semester, everyone in my class were allowed to participate in various cultural competitions and ODs were issued to anyone who wanted to participate, letting me participate in over 40 cultural festivals in a span of 12 months.

This change was brought to the college, simply because traditionally from 6th semester, people hardly respected staffs and fearing the fact that strict rules will lead to college strikes and other avoidable disturbances in College campus.

'6 second place finishes in block 'n' tackle for you, compared to Deepakh's 35 first place wins. He is on a roll.' Chris said. He was not upset, because he had never participated in Block 'n' tackle. Thanks to Hanna shifting to a foreign nation, there were places where I could actually bag a few prices. Deepakh was unbeatable on stage and was easily the best in Block 'n' Tackle, improving event by event. 'Deepakh is making some kind of record out there.'

Actually speaking cultural programs were conducted honestly over the past few months, costing Shruthi and Preethi a lot, who were not seen in various programs after losing at a stretch for a record 2 to 3 months. Thanks to them, joining hands with Jeffrey, they had lost all the luck they had. But one thing I was waiting for over the past 3 years was: to see Jeffrey on stage.

It would have took me just a matter of seconds to inform the college staff that Jeffrey was participating with girls in cultural programs, but as my parents told me long back: "how difference are you from a bastard when you make the same mistake which a bastard does!" I did not give a damn about Jeffrey and his activities. *I had better things to worry about!*

'I know.' I paused for a second and continued 'How I get to the top with just one semester left?'

'Simple.' Chris said. 'Think.'

I thought for a moment and nothing struck me. 'I have a stupid suggestion. You ready for that?'

'Carry on.'

'Shut the fuck up.'

Chris said nothing as Deepakh smiled.

'Just tell me, Deepakh.' I asked him quickly. 'How do you keep winning?'

'I donno' Deepakh confessed.

'Ok. But you must also take into consideration that he is way better than you on stage.' Chris said slowly. 'You are lucky that the people who bribe judges for various competitions, have left Block 'n' Tackle untouched for so many days, primarily because it deals with performing in front of a large audience closely observing the participants. Bad performers can't risk paying for the winning certificate. It will surely raise a few eyebrows. I would be happy if I were you.'

'You are saying that because you are not me and you don't realize that losing is better than being a mere runner up. Who will be remembered after a world cup is over?'

'The world cup winner.'

'The columns call them champions, while the loser in the finals, who would have had just one bad day on the field, will be seldom remembered.'

'I remember Brazil was the runner up in 1998 world cup.'

'Because it happened ten years back. Whom did England win against in 1970?'

'I thought they won in 1966.'

'Sorry, 1966.'

'Sorry, I don't know.'

'I rest my case.' I said. 'The team which was knocked out for its dubious performance will be remembered for a long time when compared to the runner-up of the tournament.'

'I get your point.' Chris thought and replied. 'But for you to win, you have to beat Deepakh and that Francis guy from Loyola and Abhinav from Shiva College.'

'Yes.' Deepakh agreed. 'You need to beat me.'

'And how do you intend to do that?'

'Back to square one. At the beginning of this conversation I asked you the same question.' I said. 'I don't know why I even started this discussion with you.'

'You should have thought about it when you started losing. Not when Block 'n' tackle is no more a part of any cultural. Thanks to the lack of participation in that event.'

'C'mon, there were a few participants.'

'Yeah, Deepakh, Francis, Abhinav and yourself'

'Right' And I slowly confessed to the two of them. 'I have to tell you this. Hanna is disturbing my thoughts. I was actually in love with her.'

'Ah! I get it.' Chris said to himself.

'I felt Hanna is the perfect match for me.'

'And why do you say that?'

'I still can't forget her.'

'I can't forget that you are yet to pay me my 3000 bucks that you borrowed a few months back.' Deepakh stated quickly. 'You haunt me every night'

'So you mean to say her parents had sex so that one day an asshole like you may fall in love with their daughter? Some motivation I must say!' Chris questioned me.

I looked at Chris silently for a minute as he giggled like a mad man. 'Fuck you.'

'Thank you.' Chris said. 'Ha! I got that when your Facebook status said "Love costs me my grades every semester."

'And bloody more than 20 guys liked it.' I informed. 'The highest I have got ever for any status I have put up.'

'That's the case with majority of the guys around us. So they will obviously like it.'

'You guys never shut your mouths do you?' Alvin came out and saw the three of us talking.

'That's why you never let us in, to attend any of the sessions you took over the past 3 years.' I said.

'We are now in our final year and we don't even know how your classes are!' Chris added.

'You guys never showed interest in getting into my class.' Alvin was not mad at us. *We were anyways standing outside*, I thought. We managed to just pass in all the papers, but we passed nonetheless, compared to his sincere students Param and Prasad, who did not miss any of his sessions, but flunked in all the papers. 'I am here to talk something informal to you guys.' He turned to Deepakh. 'Firstly, congrats in making your name in cultural competitions'

'Thank you, Sir.' Deepakh was happy to hear that.

'You guys ever showed interest in making a short film?' He asked us all.

'Short film?'

'Ad-Zap is good. Other programs are also equally good. But if you need to make it big and become recognized nationwide, try making a short film and send it to the national film festival and maybe you can strike gold.' He paused for a few seconds, giving us enough time to think. 'And I think you got the information that IIT Madras is conducting their cultural program this month.'

'Really?' I was shocked to get the news. 'No one informed us that St. Patrick guys were invited to participate there!'

'That's surprising. The patcult committee members were intimated almost 3 months back!'

'No wonder we did not know about it.' Chris said with disgust.

'Anyways they have a short film festival contest there. It is good for starters.'

'Sounds good.' I said. 'We'll surely think about it. Thank you sir' Alvin smiled as he left.

'Starters' I chuckled. 'That might be the last event that we might participate in during our college life.'

Chris and Deepakh nodded.

'Those patcult fuckers.' I roared in anger. 'And worse, Jim, Jeffrey's mother's father's'

'Maternal grandfather'

'Right. His maternal grandfather sister's grandson is now the representative among the 1st years for the patcult committee.'

'Do they plan it in such a way that the kids are born in Jeffrey's family after a certain time gap so that they can take up the post once the other person leaves?'

'Looks so. Long term planning'

'Patcult committee sucks. And I seriously feel bad I was desperate to join that committee a few years back.'

'If there is a Jeffrey alike in the fresher, there will be a Justin and a Chris and a Deepakh too. The legacy continues.' Chris smiled.

'And that committee has lost its value too. It is flooded with idiots who have never won outside.'

I smiled and thought for a moment. *If I actually make a movie that is worth watching, I can forward it to almost all the colleges in and around India and win from home. I will not have to struggle for a win. And honestly a good movie will be appreciated everywhere.*

'He took some time out of his busy schedule to give us this suggestion.' Chris said.

'Yeah . . . I have never thought about movie making before but it sounds interesting.'

'We can call Chitra and ask her for inputs.' Chris suggested.

'I would rather see naughty America and get better inputs.' I shouted. 'Dude this is serious. She can't dance and make us win. We have to make something really good to even stand a chance.' I continued. 'And in IIT Madras only the students from the same college can participate as a team. Inter college teams are not entertained.'

'Oh . . . no wonder all the movie stars send their kids to the same college.'

'Dude this might be the perfect finish to our eventful life in cultural events.'

'So what do you say?'

'I need to talk to Param.'

'Hmmm . . . is the IIT cultural that special?' Deepakh asked me.

'You are kidding me?' I asked Deepakh. 'It like THE THING among colleges situated in Chennai. It happens every year on a specific window, when no one else conducts their cultural and it is the one cultural people want to win.'

'Oh.'

'It matters more than all our winning certificates put together.'

'So why do you need Param for that?'

'He loves movies.'

'I know he sees movies. But does he have any experience? As in, is he a director?'

'No. An actor! He has acted in a few films.'

'What? Name some.'

'Some recent flick in Tamil called Kranti.'

'I have seen that movie. Don't remember seeing him.'

'He comes in the scene where the hero gets married.'

'Okay?'

'He was a part of the crowd blessing the couple.'

'You mean to say he is a *Rich boy*!' Chris smiled.

'Yes. His role was to sit in the front row in the marriage hall.' I said. 'Saw the scene thrice in my PC, but I still couldn't locate him. The director directing these flicks must seriously look into giving some screen space for these actors too.'

*   *   *

'I heard about your acting stint.' Chris and Deepakh were seated on the couch in my living room and Param was seated next to them. It was one of those happy days in my life when my parents had left to our native and I was let loose for a whole week. 'How do you feel after acting with Mohankanth?' Mohankanth is the superstar of Tamil cinema.

'It was tough to act with my co-star Mohankanth, but the script was well written and since we are professional actors, we were able to give one of the all-time blockbusters ever in the Tamil film industry.'

'Co-star Mohankanth?' Deepakh asked.

'Yes.'

'So much hype for a scene in which we could not even find you.' Chris giggled. 'Fucker. Try to come in front of the camera and then talk.'

'Justin, he is insulting me.' Param shouted. 'I considered your offer special and took a day off from my busy schedule to help you in your ambitious project.'

'I know'

'And here I find a movie hater Chris insult me! You know there are hundreds of directors waiting to cast me in their movies.'

'Yes.' Chris spoke. 'I will believe that. Every movie has a marriage scene. They can't leave an empty seat in the hall.'

'That's it.' Param got up from the couch. 'I am leaving.'

'Dude, Chris was joking.' I tried to cool him down. 'And I don't see any director waiting outside.' I commented. 'I'm sure you want to be seen in a proper scene. Of all the movies that you've acted in, you were one in a thousand.'

'That's because I never wanted to take someone else's screen space. I give budding stars opportunities.'

'Ah okay!' I said. 'Never mind. Here's the catch. Chris and I are planning to take part in the short film festival to be conducted in IIT. And we want you to help us make this possible.'

'A friend of mine informed me that Mohankanth's daughter is going to be the judge for the event.' Deepakh added.

'Cool.' I replied. 'So are we ready to rock the nation?'

'Yes.' Param shouted out loud. 'And I have the perfect story for a perfect short film.'

'Good.' Chris said. 'We are listening.'

'This short film will run for 7 minutes and we will need three actors.'

'Justin, you and I are 3.' Chris counted.

'Good. And all the three actors must be able to wield the camera.'

'I take my own pictures and post it on Facebook. On an average twenty guys like my pictures.' Chris said proudly. 'I know how to wield the camera.'

'A majority of them who LIKE your pictures are your mafia wars friends, who are forced to like your pictures for the pathetic energy packs you gift them!' I said.

'Dude hardly anybody likes your pictures, except Rejo, who likes everything you put up.' Chris said.

'You are right.' I replied

Param was listening. 'Now back to business.'

'Yes.' I replied. 'You have the script ready?'

'What script?'

'Oh . . .' I smiled. 'I forgot I am in India. Indians never use scripts.' I took my camera. 'So what are you planning to do?'

'I have thought about a movie on terrorism.'

'Sounds interesting' I said. 'Continue.'

'Thank you.' Param continued 'So the movie is about two of the greatest gamers in India, Justin and Deepakh, who are practicing for the national level gaming competition.'

'Hmmm . . . gaming' Chris stopped Param. 'Can I be the gamer?'

'Let him complete.' I interrupted.

'Ok.' Chris replied. 'I am gamer.'

'Shall I continue?' Param was irritated.

'Yeah, go on.' We replied in unison.

'So as I was telling, Chris is hired by a terrorist organization to kill the Justin and Deepakh.'

'Al-Qaeda!'

'Ok. Al-Queda has paid you to kill us.'

'It is Al-Qaeda!'

'Whatever. So Chris comes to Justin's place, where Justin and Deepakh are practicing in full flow. At first you come across as an innocent guy who is just curious to see how they are preparing for the competition, but later you come out of your "innocent boy" looks and kill the two of them.'

'Of all the people in this blessed world, why does Al-Qaeda have to target us gamers?' I asked. 'It sounds so lame!'

'Don't say lame, it's called being DIFFERENT. No one has ever thought about such a story before.'

'He has a point.' Chris said. 'Only THE dumbest asshole in the world will ever think of a story like this.'

'People called Einstein dumb.'

'He has a point.' I said. 'I was thinking about a script. Tell me what you think about it.'

'We are listening.'

'Ok. Chris and I are students who are making a car which can fly in the air, only to lose the car to Deepakh, who wants to sell the car to the Americans, so that they can sell it back to us.'

'Suddenly Param's story doesn't sound all that bad.' Deepakh said.

'Okay. But if you guys think otherwise, I will look into developing my script.'

'Is there any guarantee that the story will stay the same once the shoot is over?' Chris asked Param

'I don't think so.' Param replied

'I like working with Param. We did have fun when we arranged the IV for our class.' I thought about it and laughed.

'Can't wait to get started' Param said

'So here we come, movie goers.' Deepakh rose

'Wonder if mohankanth will retire after seeing our AWESOMATIC movie.'

'If he sees, he will surely retire.'

Chapter 17

Secret revealed

January 2009:

'Wait a minute.' I said to Param. 'My am I wearing formals?'

'Simply because you are gamer' Param was irritated.

Why wouldn't he? _He was the director!_

'And I thought gamers wore informal dresses.'

'Naaa . . . You would have seen that in movies.'

'No in gamezone, the most famous gaming center in Chennai.'

'I have never seen gamers wear informal.' Param clearly had no idea about gamers. Actually that was the issue Indian directors were facing. They jumped into scripts that were complex and very few did their homework in understanding how the characters that they created looked and behaved in real world. Those who did their homework became successful, and the rest lived with the scripts their assistants created. 'But if you want you can!'

'No probs. Where do I start from?'

'You come walking into the hall and Chris greets you.'

'But the scene was supposed to be like Chris joins us, right.'

'Exactly. I was just testing you, to find out whether you have devoted yourself to the movie. And believe me, you have passed!'

'I would have done a better flick.' Deepakh whispered in my ears.

'Now why should Chris wear military uniform?' I roared at Param as he brought a set of military dress and gave it to Chris.

'Cause he is a terrorist.' Param stated.

'And I thought he was working undercover.'

'He is.' Param laughed. 'That's why he is wearing Indian military uniform. To cheat the media'

'Wow! What a man!' Deepakh applauded him. 'I must say, Param is full of brains.'

'I see what you are trying to say.' I kept my hand in my head.

'Now in the next 5 hours, you will see a master piece come to life.'

'We will see.'

*   *   *

'This is one cultural program Jeffrey will regret missing. Guess his losing streak will continue.'

'And why do you say that?'

'Jeffrey and the gang have gone to Ramakrishna College. They felt they had a better chance of winning there than here in Mohammed College.'

'Who cares?' I smiled as Param came back with our ID cards. 'Our movie will be screened in exactly 30 minutes from now.'

'You think it was a good idea to submit our movie?' Deepakh asked me quickly.

'Why do you say that?'

'I read a few comments in youtube.com for our uploaded video.' I said

'Over 50 people abused our movie' Deepakh said

'And a few requested the website admin to delete the video.' Chris added

'No one requested them to see the video right.' I reminded Deepakh. 'Why did they have to volunteer to see it that they did not want to?'

'You seriously believe our movie is good?'

'I would love to say a lie. But the truth is I am sure we will be lucky if we don't leave this college with broken faces.' I said sadly. 'Let's see.'

Param smiled and did not involve him in the conversation. 'I'm eagerly waiting for the crowd's response. We will get an idea about where we stand in movie making.'

'Indian Open before the Australian Open?' Chris added.

We took a seat in the auditorium waiting for our movie to be screened.

'We will now screen the movies.' The host announced.

Nobody cheered. Only 5 of us were present in the auditorium, including the host.

'Which college are you from?' I asked the person who was seated in the auditorium with us.

'STCE'

'Super lucky dude. That is one college I wanted to get into. Neither did I have the money nor the marks.' I said.

'I will take that as a compliment.' He was not flattered. 'By the way what's happening here?'

Dude did you not hear the host's announcement.

'They're screening the movies registered for the short film contest.'

'Oh . . .' He got up from his place. 'So why are you guys here?'

'We've submitted our movie for the contest.'

'Ok.' He started walking. 'I will not risk wasting my time watching a movie here, especially one made by three idiots who call STCE GOOD. So long suckers.'

'Fuck off.' I said as the host came to me.

'Should I screen the movie or are you interested in taking the prize and leaving?'

'As in.' I was really happy. 'We won?'

'Yes. You are the only person who has submitted his movie for the contest.'

'Oh . . . You can screen the movie. We don't mind.'

'The principal has asked us not to waste electricity.'

'Ok. Then it's fine.'

'Great.' The host was relieved. 'Congrats!'

'So what do you think about our short film?'

'Since yours was the only entry we did not even see it.' The host took out three certificates and gave it to us. 'Thanks for participating.'

'We won.' Param took his certificate and roared. 'I told you my script was awesome.'

'I think we would have won even if we had have submitted an empty CD.' I was upset though I bagged the 1st prize.

'I understand.' Chris said. 'But we won. That in itself is good. And after looking at the poor participation here I think we'll have a good chance in IIT too.'

'You might be right.'

*   *   *

'You will have to submit your movie in the department before you submit any competitions.' Jeffrey demanded. 'The department staffs are angry that you have participated without informing them about what you have created. They will review your movie and decide whether the movie is eligible to be screened in any other college.'

'That ridiculous!' I replied. 'Your committee is pathetic.' I took a CD of the movie and gave it to Jeffrey. 'Here you go!'

'Thank you.' Jeffrey's eyes glittered. 'The staffs will be pleased.' He said and left.

'They have created all kind of stupid rules.' I stated to Param.

'I know.' It was our project submission day. We did not have classes on that day.

I submitted my project and the staffs appreciated me for my efforts, simply because it was done completely by Deepakh, my project mate, who surprisingly did not turn up today.

'Where is Deepakh?' I asked Chris.

'He is your partner. You must know.' Chris said. Param constantly clicked picks and recorded videos around him, giving a lame reason for his actions by labeling the upcoming months as *"the last few months of his college life!"* 'And by the way, he was sort of disturbed over the past few weeks about something.' Chris stated. 'You know what happened to him?'

'No idea.' I stated and called up Deepakh. 'He is not picking up the phone.'

'Hmmm . . . I am surprised he did not turn up even for submitting his project.' Chris said. 'Call again.'

'Ok.' I said and called up Deepakh again. 'No answer.' I said and placed my phone down only to receive a call from Deepakh again. 'Hi Deepakh. Where are you? The staffs cancelled off your viva marks and put a straight zero for not turning up today.'

'Hi Justin, this is Satyan here, Deepakh's brother.'

'Oh . . . sorry! Is Deepakh there?'

'He was not be able to come to College today because he is in the hospital now Justin.'

'What?' I roared in shock. 'What happened?'

'He got beat up by a group of goons. Nothing serious though. They will discharge him this weekend.'

'Ok' I said 'I will try meeting him today.' I informed Satyan and placed the phone down. 'You know what' I turned to Param, who was recording everything and Chris 'Deepakh is injured!'

'What?' Chris roared. 'What happened?'

'Some assholes beat him up.'

'That's surprising. I thought the guy was innocent. Did he have enemies who would actually beat?'

'That surprises me too. Let's go and check him out.'

*   *   *

'It hurts to see you like this.' I said as I took my seat next to Deepakh. Honestly, speaking Deepakh was not in a really bad shape to be upgraded to a bed in a posh private hospital. His brother informed me that Deepakh got free monthly check-up from the same hospital and so they utilized this opportunity to have the check-up and treatment done at the same time.

'It hurt me when they hit.' Deepakh said sadly.

'It will if you are alive' Chris said. Deepakh stopped discussing about Chitra after becoming a celebrity on stage.

'But tell me, bro. Who hit you?' Chris asked with interest. 'And bloody Param, switch off the bloody camera.'

'Dude, it will be fun to see this in TV in a few days, once the issue is done and dusted.'

'Not who. How many!' Deepakh cried. 'You will be surprised to hear this.'

'Tell me.'

'The reason I am here because of a guy who is madly in love with Hanna!' Deepakh said.

'Hanna?' I was shocked and so were Chris and Param. 'I thought she left for a foreign nation a year back?'

'I told her to tell you that?'

'You told her? I don't understand.'

'She is my girlfriend.' He confessed.

All of us out there were silent for a few seconds, until I finally broke the silence. 'I thought you liked Chitra . . .'

'Until I saw Hanna' Deepakh interrupted. 'On the very first meeting I got Hanna's number in MIT, we started chatting, discussing things over the phone, and eventually ended up going out together.' He said. 'It was me who made her lie to you and the rest that she was leaving to a foreign nation, simply because I feared that you will seriously go nuts about her and disturb her.'

'Oh' I was shocked. 'But she did not participate in any event SVIT'

'She upgraded herself to international level'

'Great.'

'The story does not end there.' Deepakh continued. 'She had an ex-boyfriend who was nuts about her and was actually ready to do anything to marry her. She did not like him as he was over possessive and did not let her do anything.'

'Ah! A prisoner' Chris added.

'Exactly. She needed freedom and love and I gave it to her.' Deepakh said. I felt bad hearing what he said. It hurt me to know that my very own friend had loved a girl I have been thinking about over the past few months and he had not murmured a word about her. 'Until one day.'

'Now comes the main part.' Param focused the camera straight to Deepakh's face.

'He came to know about Hanna and me, and the rest as you know is history.' Deepakh said sadly.

'And present too.' Chris said.

'So' I finally said. 'What do you intend to do about them and her?'

'You tell me.'

* * *

'This is a first of a kind!' I exclaimed.

'What?'

'Father dropping his daughter in the register office so that she can marry the person she loves.'

'That is not Hanna's father. It is her uncle.'

'Oh' I said 'She looks beautiful'

Hanna got down from the car and waved her dad goodbye. She was wearing a red silk saree, some jewelry and a string of jasmine flowers on her head. She had draped it herself, so it looked, because as she walked towards us, she stumbled upon the saree several times and almost killed herself while taking the stairs. She, nevertheless, looked like a bride ready to marry my sorry friend.

Hanna was a B.Com student from WCC (Women's Christian College) and so had completed her course last year itself and had joined a private firm. She rejected the offer from google.com to be with Deepakh, here in Chennai.

'She was always different.' Hanna came towards Deepakh and caught hold of his hand. *How I wish it was me!*

'Can we get married now?' Deepakh asked me. He looked tired and so did Hanna. It took Chris and me over one full week to arrange this runaway marriage. Thankfully Satyan and Param also helped us. It actually hurt me to think that I was actually helping Hanna marry Deepakh, when I actually would have loved to take his place!

Chitra was also present there and she wanted to see how a register marriage happened, so that she would be prepared for it, if required in the near future.

'Sure. It is 4:45 and office closes at 5.'

Deepakh came running inside with Hanna running behind him. They signed the register quickly. I signed as the witness for Deepakh and Chitra for Hanna.

'Wish you a happy married life.' I hugged Deepakh 'So what's next?'

'Complete the final semester exams.' Hanna said. 'And you mister' She told Deepakh. 'You can't stop me from doing what I want to do. We are married but are not moving in anywhere as couples.'

'Ok, honey.' Deepakh said.

Chris and I smiled at each other as they kept quarreling over something trivial. 'That is the definition of life after marriage!' Chris told me and we laughed out loud.

'When are you planning?' Chitra asked Chris.

'As quickly as possible'

Param took out his camera and clicked pictures and videos all around the place.

'You can keep the camera down and bloody join us man.' I told to Param.

'I want to record everything that is happening here.' Param replied. 'It might help us in the future.'

Chapter 18

Love Bites

January 2009:

'This is an awesome car.' Chris roared as I drove him, Deepakh and Param around the city. 'Toyota Innova is freaking awesome.' My father received a pay hike and immediately decided to upgrade my Maruti Alto to a Toyota Innova.

'Thanks bro.' I smiled. The car was smooth and it was fun driving the car. 'So tell me Deepakh. How was your first night?'

'I was in my house and she was in hers.' Deepakh said.

'Oh so you stayed back in your place and wetted your bed mat eh?' I chuckled. 'Wonder what she would have done in her place!'

'What else? Sleep tight.' Chris chuckled. 'I don't think he bought and gave her a carrot.'

'Fuck you'

'Ha ha!' I smiled. We travelled all the way to Tambaram and were enjoying every minute in my car. We

207

stopped in the bus stop next to the local railway station in Tambaram, when a well-built man came and knocked in my window and unpleasantly asked me to bring down the glass.

'Who the fuck is he?' Chris shouted.

'He looks like a goon.' I said and did not open the window. Another sturdy well-built guy came and hit the window next to Param, who was seated in the passenger seat. 'Don't open the window.'

'I don't think they will wait for that.' Param roared as one of them picked up a stick and broke my window glass.

'Fuck' I roared and put my head down.

'Open the door fucker.' One of them roared and opened the door and got in. One thing I realized in India was that when something took place here, people stood and watched. I was sure that everyone had seen the goons break my glass but none of them came forward to help us.

'Who are you guys and what do you want?' I cried.

'Your friend Deepakh knows us.' One of them sat next to him and said. 'Take the car straight to the place where I instruct you to. There is someone who wants to meet you guys there.'

'Smile please.' Param switched on his camera and recorded it.

*   *   *

'Welcome my dear friends.' I drove myself and everyone, in my car, to a house, situated in a street in Tambaram, almost a kilometer drive from the railway station. We were made to sit inside an empty hall, surrounded by 4 goons who were clearly paid to threaten and kick our ass. 'Nice to see you guys.'

'Nice to see you, sir.' Param said. 'Smile please.' He took his camera and clicked. Surprisingly, the guy who spoke smiled. He was clearly not a goon. He looked like a person of the same age as me. But he was well-built and clearly spent hours in the gym. He had a French beard and he looked scary.

'Will that do?'

'Yes. Can I record what is going to happen here?'

'That won't be necessary. I will do that for you.' He borrowed Param's camera and focused on us. 'Please start.'

He instructed the goons. All of them came and hit us.

'Who are you guys?'

'He is Rocky.' Deepakh said. 'Hanna's ex-boyfriend.' Deepakh turned towards Rocky 'I already got nice shots from your guys some days back. Why again?'

'My marriage gift to you.' He smiled. 'You know I loved her so much, right?'

'Right'

'Then why the fuck did you marry her?'

'Because she married me.'

'You came into her life and took her away from me.' He roared.

'All was well before he got into your life.' I felt my bones breaking. 'Hit him, leave us.'

'You guys arranged the marriage. Thank you.' Rocky roared.

'Am I visible in the video?' Param asked Rocky.

'I must say the clarity is really good.' He smiled. 'I am impressed. I must get one of those.'

'Please do that . . . ah . . . . It is the . . . . ohhh . . . . best camera in the . . . . Oh . . . . Market now.'

'It is now all over right?' I asked Rocky, as a goon hit in my ass. 'Why do you hit us now?'

'Personal satisfaction.' Rocky stated. 'And above all I am a local goon. So I must hit someone once in a while to keep my guys occupied.'

'Valid.'

*   *   *

'Dad, I will not be coming tonight.'

'What happened?'

'Some project work. Chris and I will be staying back in Deepakh's place.'

'Fine with me.' My father switched off the mobile. 'Man, it hurts. He looked like a college kid' I said as I placed my hand in my broken limbs. We were seated in the road side in Saidapet. They left us after spending 3 hours beating us up. 'What does he do?'

'He is a college kid.'

'Kid?'

'He is pursuing MSc in Loyola College with Mathematics as his specialization.' He said. 'He has a few paid goons surrounding him all the time.'

'Ah! Man I must say, it hurts.' I cried. 'And what hurts me more is the broken window in my car. How will I drive it back home?'

'Driving?' Chris answered.

'Fuck you.' I said.

'You know' Deepakh said 'Someone told me once. You don't gain anything by losing something.'

'The videos have come out well.' Param said. 'Chris, you must see Justin's expression when he was beaten up by that goon who targeted only me.'

'Show me.' Chris moved across to Param and checked it. 'Nice. You need to upload it in youtube.com and share the link in Facebook. It seriously looks good.'

'Sorry guys.' Deepakh said.

'No issues, man. It was more like a massage to me.' Chris lied.

'I can see that. You were the only one who was crying there.' I said.

'Pain and tears go hand in hand. I cannot do anything about that.' Chris said.

'But you know what' I added 'That fucker said that he will not intervene in your life. He just wanted us to realize how much it hurt him.'

Deepakh picked up his phone and started conversing with Hanna. 'Please be silent. I don't want her to know anything that happened out here.'

*   *   *

'Yes . . . . Exactly . . . . I will do that . . . . No not needed . . . . They are idiots . . . . You don't want to fight with dogs . . . . Not needed . . . . Seriously . . . .' The news spread and everyone was shocked about what they heard. Actually no one was bothered about the reason why we were beaten up. The only issue thing everyone was concerned about us: *how could they hit our college guy.* And people I was talking about were none other than my college guys.

'Let's show who we are' Chacko called me up and told us to bring Rocky to Besant Nagar, where my college guys, a promised number of 50 guys minimum would be waiting for payback.

'I have Rocky's number.' Deepakh informed. 'Let me call him and bring him there. It's payback time.'

*   *   *

'Where are our guys?' I asked Deepakh as we landed in Besant Nagar. As promised, we expected 50 to be there, but surprisingly there weren't any there. They ditched us. I turned and saw a Maruti Van coming our way.

'Message Chacko and ask where our class guys'

Where are you guys? I messaged Chacko and waited as the Rocky's car closed on us. Param shot the scene and smiled.

'Feels like I am acting in a movie.'

Sorry man. We had to drop in in Raman's house for his sister's wedding. We will be joining you shortly, in let's say an hour or two. I got the reply, as Rocky's car stopped.

'What does the message say?' Chris asked Deepakh.

'It indirectly says: RUN!'

'So what do we do?'

'RUN!' I jumped into my car as Rocky came running to my car with a hockey stick with his group of goons.

'Let me in' roared Param

I took my car out of the place and ran away, as a heavy blow hit my car. 'What the fuck was that?'

'Wait let me see.' Chris looked out. 'He broke your side mirror and back light with his hockey stick. He aims well.'

'Fuck!' I cried. 'I am so dead. Double fuck.'

Chapter 19

Short Film

March 2009:

'Would you like to see the movie I did?'

'What is it about?'

'About everything that happened because of Deepakh'

'Not today. As today is THE DAY!' I said as I found myself among 50000 other students in IIT Madras for their annual cultural program *"Daarang"*, the one place where people from all around the world come to participate. It was also the hunting ground for desperate boys in search of desperate girls.

Our wounds were slowly healing and we were able to finally walk. My father grounded me for a few days and banned me from using the car again.

'I know.' Chris replied.

'Jeffrey said it is the college's responsibility to submit the movie here in IIT Madras. You think he would have done that?'

'I did' Jeffrey arrived in the venue with his gang. 'Though I did not want to'

'Thanks' I said and turned away from Jeffrey. He in turn walked off with a cheeky smile.

'I think he has done something really wrong.' Chris stated. 'I don't like his smile.'

'If he has not done anything wrong, I think we bag a prize in movie making. By the way Param is describing our movie, I think it has all the ingredients of being a runaway hit among the jury members.' Deepakh said.

'They are not the jury members. They are a few guys who thought this IIT campus was some random vintage tourist spot.'

'Oh'

'You did not see the movie?' I asked Deepakh.

'I did'

'I will not say that!' I smiled. 'Anyways, anytime now they will be calling us.'

"WE WOULD LIKE TO HAVE JEFFREY'S TEAM TO COME TO THE REVIEWING ROOM." The speaker was loud.

'What?'

'I never knew he was participating in this competition.' I said.

'We are participating.' Jerome came in and walked towards the room. 'Thanks for the video.'

'What?' I was thunder struck.

'Ha ha!' He smiled. Param looked shocked and started crying.

'They might call us to sign a contract with Mohankanth to help him make his next flick.' Jerome replied. 'Heard your movie is that good!'

'Just get lost' I roared, as Deepakh and Chris said nothing and stood silently, as Jerome and Jeffrey walked into the room. 'These guys, I hate them. The country does not need people like this.'

'What to do? There are millions of them.' Chris said sadly.

'But you know what. I am not sad.' I said. 'And I donno why!'

'I know why.' Param suddenly got up from his place. 'Cause we can still participate.' He showed his CD. 'We can submit this.'

* * *

We walked into the room where Mohankanth's daughter, a few volunteers and a panel of judges were seated.

'Hi. I am Jeffrey. I directed the movie and I take full credit for everything you saw.' Jeffrey spoke quickly. 'Where is the contract paper?'

'Fucker.' I said to myself

'Credit for giving an empty CD?' The judge asked.

'Empty CD?'

'Yes. The CD you submitted is empty.' One of the panelists said. 'Do you have a backup CD?'

'No.' I looked hard at Param. I felt like I had a knife in my hand, as Jeffrey started shivering.

'You did not write the movie properly, did you?'

'I think so.'

'Thank God.'

'Sorry. Did you guys upload the movie on YouTube?'

'Yes. Thank god.' Jeffrey roared as he went to the machine and played the movie.

'How did he know the link to the video in youtube?' Chris asked me.

'I told him when I submitted the movie.'

'Oh'

'Here you go. Sit back and enjoy.'

The movie started and the speakers were kept in full volume. The video was not clear as it was in mp4 format, but worse it had no music.

'No background music?' The panelist asked Jeffrey, as the panelists murmured among themselves. 'You uploaded our movie without the background score.'

'Look at the bottom of the video.' I looked at the link and there was a note added which read "NOT AUTHORISED TO USE THE MUSIC WITHOUT COPYRIGHTS."

'So long for the prize.' I chuckled said as Jerome and Joshua gravely sunk into their chairs because of the flop show. 'They ended up putting up a flop show. So much for cheaters.'

'Cheaters never prosper'

'The movie is bad.' Mohankanth's daughter stated. 'Believe me, it is really bad.'

'Hmmm . . .' Jeffrey roared. 'How can you say that?'

She got up from the place and said 'Let me explain, kid.' She sounded polite. 'I understand YouTube has some policies because of which the sound was deleted from the flick. But let me explain where your movie went wrong.'

'Please do that.'

'A guy says he is their college mate and comes to their house to play a game, only to kill them because they are going to participate in a gaming contest in Delhi? Am I right?'

'I told Param the story sucked.' I whispered to Chris.

'Yes, isn't it different?'

'Story sucks. Movie sucks even more.' She continued. 'Now about where you have gone wrong, let me explain it to you. Your friend, the so called terrorist, comes from Afghanistan to kill, and the first scene shows your friend sitting in an Indian toilet with a sign board that reads Afghanistan.'

'We can't afford to go to Afghanistan.'

'But you could have chosen a better location to show it was Afghanistan. Of all the places in a house, why the hell did you choose a toilet?' She replied. 'And then the gamers and the terrorist in the second scene discuss about their school and college life. How could they have been together for 18 years?'

'He was sent to India when he was as young as 2 years old so that he can kill them once they grow and become prepared to participate in the competition. LONG TERM PLANNING!'

'I won't buy that.' I told Chris. 'That's the shittiest justification. Bloody bugger, this Param.'

'Alright' she replied. 'And do you want me to point out many more mistakes.' She asked politely.

'One will do.' Jeffrey replied. 'And thank you for letting them know.'

'And your movie will not be screened.' One of the volunteers stated as he handed over the empty CD to Jeffrey.

'I think she understand movies.' I chuckled, accepting the fact that our movie was bad. Though the movie was submitted by Jeffrey, Param felt bad that the movie received negative reviews.

'Seriously dude.' I kept my hand on Param's shoulder and said 'She knew everything about what it takes for a movie to be good.'

'So what do we do with the CD?' Chris asked Jeffrey. 'May I keep it?'

'Fuck off.' Jeffrey shouted, as he stepped out of the hall.

'Cool. I needed one.'

'Oh yeah! They asked us to submit a CD in college, so that they can use it to give us the details required to carry forward the summer project.'

'No. I need this CD to copy and keep a backup for all the porn movies in my system.'

'You guys did it intentionally, didn't you?'

'God is with us.' Deepakh smiled.

I said nothing.

"PARAM's TEAM CAN COME NEXT AND PLAY THEIR VIDEO."

Param walked forward and put the CD.

'Hope this works.' I whispered.

The movie started with I conversing over the phone with Deepakh, then meeting Deepakh in the hospital, then the marriage scene, then the bash up scene and finally the escape scene.

'Awesome.' Mohankanth's daughter said. 'I am impressed.'

'Thank you.'

'Though the actors are the same who performed in that pathetic movie Jeffrey submitted, you guys have shown your mettle in this movie.' She appreciated us.

'Thank you'

'The goons looked real'

'They sure do'

'I have some good news for you.'

'Tell us' Chris said eagerly.

'This movie is going to the nationals for the heart it has.'

'Whoa!' I roared in joy and so did Deepakh, Param and Chris.

'What do you call it?'

'Love bites!'

*   *   *

'20k bucks, a prestigious award from IIT Madras, recognition'

'Yes'

'And we made it to the national film making competition.'

'Thanks to Hanna and me' Deepakh said proudly.

'And Rocky too. He handled the camera really well.'

'Hi' Two chicks came in and stood next to me. They were covered in white shirt and blue jeans. Both were fair and thin. They looked conscious with respect to their diet and maintained their curves with perfection. They had long black hair and looked too good. They were covered with ornaments. But the only talking point that could have been against them would have been their accent. The girl who said "*hi*" had a mallu accent written all over their "*HI*"

'Hi' I said happily.

'I am Sarah and this is Shreya. We saw your movie. It was really nice.' Sarah said.

'Thank you'

'We are actually 3rd year students pursuing our B.Com in WCC College.'

'Ok' Param came in front and smiled.

'Can you help us make a movie like that?'

'Ok' I smiled 'If you guys agree to have a cup of coffee with us.'

Sarah thought for a moment. *Did I jump the gun?* But surprisingly she smiled. 'Sure'

Chapter 20

The End—Maybe

April 2009:

I fell in love with Sarah and luckily she also accepted me. I informed my parents about her and taking into consideration that she was from Cochin (Kerala) and a mallu catholic, all went well and both families decided to join hands.

Param left for IIMC, Delhi and had decided to pursue a career in film making. Jeffrey and his gang were placed in HCL Technologies and we were sure that they were going to kill everyone there with their mischievous ways. Actually the reason why they got into HCL was because Jeremiah was working there and interviewed Jeffrey during the campus recruitment drive.

Deepakh was placed in Infosys and revealed to his parents that he had tied the knot with Hanna and though they initially were not ready to accept the couple, within days the couple convinced their family and took a house in Tambaram and stayed there. The house that they took was the same place where we were beaten up by Rocky and his gang. Actually he was the one who helped them to get that house, after Param helped him get into movies as a body double for action sequences.

Chitra took over her NGO and travelled to Dubai to find sponsors.

Chris and I joined an event management company in Mumbai and decided to shift to the business capital of India.

'So this is the end, huh?' Chris asked.

'Yes.' I said as I boarded the train with him. 'For now!'

'Hmmm! The journey was good.' Chris stated.

'As they say "Reaching the destination was never the prize, but the journey travelled is."' I smiled. 'And you know what? I have created a list of activities that we need to do in the company.'

'Tell me.'

'Not now.' I smiled. 'Maybe in a year or two'

Herbert is a marketing student from Loyola Institute Of Business Administration. A desi movie buff, and a western theater enthusiast, Herbert loves travelling across the globe. He has worked previously as a freelancer, making teaser videos for movies and companies across the globe. He is presently working in an IT firm as a project manager in Chennai, India